THREE MEN IN
NEW SUITS

by

J. B. PRIESTLEY

THE BOOK CLUB
121 Charing Cross Road, London, W.C.2

FIRST PUBLISHED APRIL 1945
SECOND IMPRESSION MAY 1945
THIRD IMPRESSION JULY 1946

BOOK
PRODUCTION
WAR ECONOMY
STANDARD

PRINTED AND BOUND IN GREAT BRITAIN BY
THE HOLLEN STREET PRESS, LTD., LONDON, W.1

AUTHOR'S NOTE

THIS novel was written and printed some time before the European War ended and demobilisation began in earnest. At that time I was under the impression that demobilised soldiers were to receive the " utility suits " that had been so unpopular with civilians. This is not the case, and since then I have had the opportunity of inspecting the civilian outfits given to demobilised officers and men of all Services, and I was delighted to find that these out- fits are of excellent quality. The whole scheme, in fact, does credit to the Services and the Ministry of Supply, and I beg the reader to ignore the references to the de- mobilised men's suits in my novel. And this warning can be my apology to those officials, in the above departments, whose actual plans have shown so much good sense and imagination.

J. B. P.

THREE MEN IN NEW SUITS

I

It was quiet in the Saloon Bar of the *Crown*, that after-noon. The lunch-hour rush was over. Only twenty minutes now from closing-time. The barmaid, a middle-aged woman who had come down to Lambury from London during the flying-bomb period and was chiefly busy now wondering how she could get back to London, wiped the bar counter and then stared at the mild Spring sunlight in the Market Square. There were only four customers in the Saloon : an elderly man who was peering dubiously at a newspaper, which he had folded into the smallest possible reading space, as if it were a secret document ; another elderly man, who was smoking a pipe and gazing at the opposite wall ; and two girls, giggling together in a corner, bold lively pieces wearing trousers and bright scarves, probably from the aircraft factory.

Perhaps because she was waiting anxiously for closing-time, the barmaid suddenly felt that everybody and everything there—the four customers, the bar, the *Crown*, the Market Square, all Lambury, the very sunlight itself—were waiting for something. What that some-thing was, she didn't know. Probably nobody did. But that was the feeling she had, and she felt it so strongly that she decided to tell her friend about it at tea-time. Perhaps it was just the end of the war. Here it was—and now—what next? That was it. What next?

One of the girls—the Spanish type with the mustard scarf and too much dark red lipstick—looked across and winked. The barmaid felt her face cracking into a professional answering smile. Then she looked away, quickly, decisively. Nothing to wink about. In fact,

1

there was plenty not to wink about. For instance, the way that kid had been in and out of this bar all the winter, with this chap and that one, all sorts, swallowing gins-and-limes, talking at the top of her voice, doing a film-star act. Well, they were paying them off now at the aircraft factory. Probably these two had just about finished. Kids like these would soon have to knuckle down a bit. Do them good too. The barmaid found herself feeling old, resentful, sour, knew she was not really like that, and so was annoyed.

A lorry in the square set its engine shuddering and rattling, then went roaring away. The silence that followed seemed unfathomable. Some kind of exhaustion seeped through into the Saloon Bar of the *Crown*. The elderly man with the folded newspaper now stared at nothing, as if he had done with newspapers for ever. The two girls stopped whispering and giggling, and one looked blank and the other looked suddenly melancholy. The barmaid leaned on a plump elbow and waited for time to pass.

Then it was all different. Three young men in new suits came in. The suits were blue, grey and brown ; but were alike in being severely, even skimpily, cut, and in being very new. The young men who wore them— and wore them newly too—were not alike, for one was tallish, fair, good-looking, another was of similar height but dark and beaky, and the third was burly and bat- tered ; yet there was a distinct likeness between them, as if all three had come from the same place and had been doing the same things there. And they brought with them a sharpened and hard masculinity, which acted instantly upon the two girls like a dig in the ribs. The barmaid felt its influence too but was uncertain in her reception of it. She smiled uncertainly.

" What's it to be? " asked the tallish, fair, good-looking

one, who wore the blue suit. He had an educated voice, officer type.

" What 'ave they got? " the burly, brown-suited one demanded. He talked with the local burr.

" Brown ale," suggested the barmaid.

" Three halves then," said the dark one in the grey suit. He had the local burr too, but was not so rough as the other. But he had small, rather deep-sunken eyes above that beak of a nose, and the barmaid did not much care for the look of him. While she drew the beer she could hear the two aircraft girls talking and giggling again, showing off. Trust them!

" Well," said the nice-looking blue suit, " here we are. Lambury."

" Here we are." This was the beaky one.

" That's right," said burly brown vaguely, looking about him a bit.

The barmaid put the three beers in front of them. " You boys just out of the army? "

" That's right," the burly brown one repeated, in exactly the same tone of voice as before.

If there was anything more to say on this subject, nobody thought of saying it.

" How's Lambury? " asked the good-looking one, with a glint of mockery in his bright blue eyes.

The barmaid didn't propose to have herself saddled with Lambury. She was from London and hoping to get back there as soon as possible, she told them. Lambury might be all right for them who liked it.

" Well, we like it—don't we, chaps? "

" Anyhow, what's wrong with it? " the dark beaky fellow demanded, almost rudely.

" I didn't say there was anything wrong with it," said the barmaid. " Do you live here? "

" No. We've a farm—Crowfield way."

3

" That's where I live—Crowfield," the one in the brown suit, the rough thick-set one, told her.

" Bus goes that way, doesn't it? In about ten minutes time, eh? " This was the beaky one again, the one who came from a farm but didn't look like it.

The barmaid didn't know, and added, with a touch of Cockney contempt, that she never knew where the local buses went.

" Well, it does. That's the bus we're waiting for."

This was from the saucy girl with the mustard scarf, who now said she wanted a packet of Players, though what she really wanted—the barmaid told herself—was to get talking to these chaps.

" We know about that bus all right," the girl continued, " because it goes near the factory where we work. It starts from the other side of the square." She looked from one to the other of the three young men with bold dark eyes. They stared back at her, like sailors on some far tropical shore.

The blue boy, the good-looking one, who seemed to have most about him, broke the spell. " Thank you. I'm not going that way myself but these two are. Are you taking that bus? "

" Yes, we are." She indicated the other girl, who now looked haughty and aloof.

" There you are, Herbert—Moldie. Nice company on the way too. Have a drink. You've just time." He turned to include the other girl, who pushed out her lower lip and shook her head.

" Well, I will even if you won't, Edie," cried the dark girl. " Small gin-and-lime, please." She offered them her packet of Players.

" Aircraft factory, isn't it? " asked the beaky fellow, looking at the girl severely.

She gave him a saucy glance. " Yes. D'you mind? "

4

" No. Why should I mind? "

" Well, you looked as if I thought I ought to apologise or something. Perhaps you think we've all been sitting there varnishing our fingernails and getting twelve quid a week for doing it."

The one in the brown suit gaped at her. Blue suit grinned, might even have winked. But big nose in the grey suit still stared—and he had small angry eyes—and did not even smile. " I didn't think," he told her. " Haven't started thinking yet. What's the matter with you? "

" Now, now, now! " And the blue-suited one included them all in a rich warming smile. Even the barmaid found it hard to resist. " No sharp tempers, please. We may all lose our tempers soon, but that's no reason to start now. Let me sort out the party for you. This stern chap, who used to be a corporal in the Banfordshire Light Infantry but is now returning to his father's farm, is Herbert Kenford. This one, also of the Banfordshires, is Eddie Mold—married, by the way—eh, Eddie? Herbert isn't—and that's probably why he's being so stern with you. I don't come into the picture really—I'm going to Swansford, in a car with any luck—but my name's Alan Strete——"

" And you come from Swansford Manor then," said the girl, surprisingly. " Officer, I suppose, eh? "

" No, a sergeant. Didn't think you'd know my family."

" I don't, but I've heard of 'em. My name's Doris Morgan. And my friend there is Edie Young."

" And there we are then," said Strete amiably. " Everybody knows everybody."

" Farmers haven't done so badly, y'know." And Doris looked defiantly at Herbert Kenford again, as if for the last two minutes they had been having a silent but fierce

5

argument. " In fact, most of 'em have made a packet. And I never saw twelve quid a week or anything like it. And, mostly, I split my nails."

" Turn it up, will you," said Herbert Kenford. " You're not arguing with me. You're arguing with yourself. What's the matter with you? "

" We don't understand you, Doris." And Strete gave a mocking sketch of a sigh. " We're just three chaps who want a bit of peace and quiet—no harm in us at all."

" And you think you're going to get some peace and quiet now, do you? " she demanded, quite fiercely.

" Doris, stop it," the other girl called.

" That's what we have in mind. Isn't it, Moldie? "

" Suit me all right," the man Mold muttered. He was no talker, evidently. The girl ignored him, and stared defiantly again at Kenford.

" I'll tell you what's the matter with me. Some chaps like you came in here the other night, straight out of the army, and started throwing their weight about. They'd done it all, for a bob or two, while we'd sat about, pretending to work, waiting till the whistle went so we could find the nearest American and go on a blind, and collected about ten or twelve quid a week for doing it. They had it all taped. You couldn't tell 'em anything. I couldn't even tell 'em we were being paid off at the factory, that we'd earned what we got, that I used to work in a shop and it isn't there any longer, that we had a nice house in Croydon and that isn't there any longer neither——"

" We had a nice battalion once too," said Strete, and now his smile was no longer rich and warming. " Didn't we, Herbert? "

" Let her finish, Alan. I want to know what's wrong with her and what she's getting at."

But she looked across at Strete this time. " All right,

you've had it. But we haven't been living on the moon, y'know. I had two brothers once——"

"I see," said Strete gently. "But you needn't take it out of us, you know."

"No," she cried, "and don't you take it out of us either. That's all."

"But look," said Kenford, with a weary patience that was almost insulting. "Nobody's taking it out of you. Not one of us had said anything to you. If you're in a bad temper, as you seem to be, then don't try and work it off on us. See?"

They stared at each other, and it was the girl who looked away at first. In fact, she blushed. And then turned sulky. "All right. I'm talking out of my turn I expect—as usual. Only—when you do start thinking— just get it right."

"Get what right?"

"Everything. You'll see. The bus'll be there now, if you want to catch it. Come on, Edie."

At that moment, as she made a move, there was a screech of old brakes outside, and then the door opened to admit, hurriedly but splendidly, a large figure in uniform. The girls stared and then fled.

"Alan!"

"Gerald! Mother got my wire?"

"Just in time for me to make it. Any chance of a quick one for the road?"

"You'll just manage it," said the barmaid, and made haste to give him the double whisky he demanded.

"Two of our chaps, Gerald. Been with me all the time. Herbert Kenford. Eddie Mold. My brother— Gerald—still a major on the Staff—but what the hell do we care now!"

Gerald grinned broadly, gave them a huge friendly hand, and said vaguely that he hoped they would find everything all right at home.

" Better be making for that bus," said Kenford. " Come on, Eddie. We're on the telephone at home, Alan, if you want to arrange for us to meet sometime."

" Of course I do, Herbert. And be careful of that girl," he called. " I think she has her eye on you—though for what I wouldn't know."

Eddie Mold guffawed, but Herbert said nothing. Gerald grinned at their backs, then kept the grin on for Alan and the barmaid. " If it's the one with the yellow scarf, he might do worse—he might do a lot worse. What do you say? "

" He might do a lot better," said the barmaid, removing the glasses. " Time now, please, gentlemen. Time ! "

She went to the door, to lock up, a few moments after they had gone, and through the pane of glass in the door, from which most of the blue paint had vanished, she saw the two men—the bulging, red-necked major and his slighter brother in the new blue suit—dive into the car and depart. Across the square the bus that had swallowed the other four was moving off. There was still enough paint on the glass to blur the scene outside and to take much of the colour out of it. Like a bit of a dullish film, she thought. Behind her the bar was settling into its usual afternoon staleness and exhaustion. She felt like that herself. Sad in a silly sort of way too. Better than being bad-tempered, though, as so many seemed to be now. What she had to do, she decided once again, was to get back to London, sharp as she could. Nothing ever really happened down here.

2

As he drove, Gerald was talking about the car. He had always liked to talk about cars. "She won't pull, of course," he was saying. "This petrol knocks hell out of the cylinders. Just muck, really."

Alan listened to him, with affection too, for he was fond of old Gerald, but he was giving him only a fraction of his attention. He was watching the well-remembered countryside flow past, now with the tender bloom of Spring on it. The ancient magic was working.

"Wonderful country this, y'know, Gerald. Look at those beeches."

"Right, old boy. Nothing to beat it. Remember when I first came back from the desert, I walked round like a man in a bloody dream. Got used to it now, of course."

They turned into the Swansford road, which was still little more than a wandering lane. It went by like a lovely old tune. The blackthorn was out; birds were calling; and the afternoon was warm gold in the little valley. Like the title of an old film shakily focused on the screen, there came again, somewhere at the back of Alan's mind, the vague first stirring of that Arcadian dream which for ever haunts the imagination of the English. He recognised it, tried to dismiss it, thought about it.

"I suppose that's why we never settle down to build cities properly," he said.

"What, old boy?" Then Gerald laughed. "Ought to have remembered you had that trick. Sort of talking to yourself. Don't bother telling me, my lad. By the way, did I tell you that Ann and the kids are at the house. Diana's there too. Quite a party."

" Uncle Rodney? "

" Of course. No stamps, though. He's sold the whole dam' lot—got a fat price too. Wouldn't believe it at first when he told me. Didn't think people were so barmy. But they are—they are. I ought to have known."

" What's he collecting now? " asked Alan.

" Can't decide. At least, hadn't decided up to last night. You must show him that suit, and tell me what he says if I don't happen to be there. God, he'll hate it." Gerald laughed. He had to slow down now behind a farm cart. " Bit of a stinker, though, isn't it? That's what you get for not taking a commission and doin' this sergeant act of yours. How was it, old boy, stickin' it out as a sergeant? "

" All right. But only because I managed to keep with the same old outfit."

" Quite. Know how you felt. Mother and the girls didn't understand, of course. No reason why they should. But they'll stop arguing now you're out. They're busy now thinking of a nice girl for you to marry. Heard 'em at it last night. Want a nice girl to marry? "

" Not just now, thanks, Gerald. Lots left over, I suppose."

" Lots an' lots," Gerald said. " Usual thing. Dam' shame too. You'll have to do your duty. After you've looked round a bit, of course."

" How is Ann? " They were turning into the drive now, and Alan noticed that Gerald had slowed down even more than was necessary, as if he wanted to say a final word or two before they reached the house.

" She's in great form. Plannin' like mad, of course, the way they do, though I keep telling her it's too early. And the kids have been talking about you for days. They think you're the real soldier—Uncle Alan will tell us all about it, won't he?—you know—and I don't say they haven't the right idea there. Look old boy—go easy with Di."

" What's the matter with her? " Alan could guess, but he wanted Gerald to tell him.

" She's a bit on edge, of course," Gerald said. " Only to be expected. I'm back. And now you're back. And her bloke's not—and never will be. What got her down was this long *Missing* business—you know, believing for months he'd turn up somehow, and then finally being told, not only by the Air Ministry but also by one of the lads in his crew who did get back, that he'd had it all right. Well, it's made her rather bitter. And she's not getting on too well with Mother. You were always thicker with Di than I was, so if you can do anything, Alan, I hope you will. In the meantime—you know, old boy, don't need to tell *you*—just go easy. Well, here we are, such as it is."

The sight of the old house split Alan into two men. One, who had been born there, recognised with affection every window pane and worn brick, and simply came home. The other, who had been away for years and had fought his way from the African desert into the middle of Europe, stared at this rambling old building, huddled deep into its green island hillside, and began to wonder what this remote place meant to him. If one man came home, the other still arrived at a billet at the end of a long march. Sergeant Strete of the Banfordshires had come from his Army Group. And young Alan Strete, younger son of Lady Strete and the late Sir William, of Swansford Manor, had come home. This split, this sudden double vision, was more than confusing. He felt a deep distress. This was really a case of pulling yourself together. And he had to do it at once.

" You look wonderful, darling," said his mother, " but where did you get that terrible suit? It reminds me of somebody absurd we had here lately. Who was it? "

Diana remembered. " It was the man who came about the coal. All right, Alan, you don't look a bit like him. Only his clothes were rather like yours. He must have been dressed in his best Utility."

" Is that what this suit is? " his mother asked, smiling, as if Diana and he had persuaded her to join in some childish game.

" That's what it was," said Alan. " The ones the civilians didn't want. We've all got them. And anyhow, if I minded it, which I don't, it doesn't matter because I can soon change into some of my old things."

" Well, I don't know," his mother said doubtfully, " there aren't many things left. You'll see when you go up—yes, the same old room, darling." She smiled.

She did not look much older. There was something unchanging about her. It was Diana who gave him a shock. All her youth had gone ; she looked brittle and chalky ; and although she smiled when the others did, and her voice was pleasant enough, if without the old warmth, her eyes never seemed to meet his but slipped away as if there was some unresolved quarrel between them. It made Alan wonder if he had ever said something about her husband, Derek—not a chap he had ever cared much about—that Diana was remembering now, holding against him. It couldn't be just because he had come back and Derek hadn't.

" All the billetees and evacuees went months ago, of course," his mother was saying, " but we still can't get much done—though Burchell promises to put us first"——

" He says that to everybody," Diana put in.

" Don't interrupt, darling, because the last thing I want to do at this moment is to talk to poor Alan about Burchell—and I only mentioned him and not being able to get things done yet, because I wanted to make Alan understand that this house is still far from being really comfortable and we can't help it still looking rather piggy——"

"Nonsense, Mother it all looks perfect," Alan cried, glancing brightly about him. They were still standing in the long low hall, where the afternoon light was mellowed into almost a rich dusk, relieved by the glowing flowers, the gleam of brass, the mirroring surfaces of the old polished wood. There was nothing there he didn't remember, yet the total effect, arriving at the end of a sergeant's last journey, made him marvel.

"We're still not using the drawing-room," said his mother. "Tea will be in the old nursery. And quite soon too. Diana, go up with Alan."

On the first landing, out of the carved Spanish oak wardrobe (still with its old Armada galleon look), Mrs. Hake appeared, like a female troll. For a moment it was strange to find himself towering above her, smiling down at her crinkling old face. She couldn't be a day less than seventy, might be more. How they'd kept her running about for them!

"Well, this is one day I can thank Him for," cried Mrs. Hake, who lived in a cosy medieval universe. "Now, no more soldiering, eh, Mr. Alan?"

"Not if I can help it." Yes, she was old and rapidly dwindling, and ought to have been taking it easy years ago. Or would she just die now if she left the family, living as she did her life through theirs? Diana would know.

Mrs. Hake insisted upon showing him his room, and he might have just come home from school. "All your bits o' things," she announced proudly. "And try not to mess it all up as you used to do, Mr. Alan, 'cos I don't get the help I did. Miss Diana'll tell you that. What have you done with your soldier clothes?"

" Left 'em behind."

" Well, I can't say I'm sorry, specially them 'eavy boots churning everything up. But I expect you two want to talk, like you always did." And she left them.

He sat on the bed and Diana sat in the little basket chair, just as they had always done when he came home. He lit a pipe, blew a little cloud of smoke in her direction, then looked at her expectantly through it. Because for a few moments they did not speak, time ran back for them, and all was as it had been. Then Diana tightened her lips, as if deliberately and rather painfully dragging herself into the present, and raised her fine dark eyebrows at him.

" Bathroom," she announced, almost as if he were a new guest. " You'll have to share Old Monster with Uncle Rodney and me. Mother has hers, of course. And Gerald and Ann and family have claimed the new one. Ann's hardly ever out of it—she stays in there half the morning, and then takes hours and hours with the children in the evening—really, it's maddening."

" Never mind Ann. And anyhow I've always had Old Monster." It was their antique bathroom, wheezy in its old age, with a great high bath like a giant's coffin, and it kept you waiting in its cold desert spaces.

" Yes, but don't forget Uncle Rodney. He takes ages."

" Where is he, by the way? "

" In his room, playing the gramophone." And Diana didn't even smile.

" He hasn't taken to playing the gramophone, has he? "

" Yes, it's his latest. He read somewhere that certain pieces of music are really elegies to a dying civilisation—I think Ernest Newman said it—and now he plays them over and over. Honestly, you know, Alan ! "

He laughed. " Come on, Di. That's pretty funny. Good old Rodney ! "

14

But she shook her head. "You'll stop thinking it's funny after you've been back a week or two," she said crossly. "I'm tired of Uncle Rodney. And Mother's nearly as bad."

He refused to be drawn into this. It was too soon. He looked about him again, and two large photographs on the wall caught his eye. "School cricket," he said, more to himself than to her. "Queer, y'know. I never particularly wanted to be in the eleven. I never wanted to have a photograph of it. And I definitely never wanted to be the kind of chap who keeps such photographs hanging on his wall. Yet there they are. Hang it, Di, we must be mechanisms half our time, automata, jolly robots—um?"

She considered this for a moment. "I think men are—more than women. Look at Gerald."

"Well, what about Ann?"

"No, Ann's not like that—she's rather appalling, of course—but not like that. To begin with, she's full of plans all the time."

This was better, more like the old Diana. Alan encouraged it. "Yes, but the plans are probably automatic—sort of conditioned reflexes. I'd back old Gerald against her—because now and then he does do or say something quite unexpected—and she never does. Or she didn't."

"She still doesn't. As a matter of fact, she's far more insensitive than poor old Gerald—her kind of woman is just more insensitive than anybody. God, she makes me angry. She just won't understand about—about Derek and me—I mean, the way I feel about him. She doesn't seem to understand there may be something very special about a relationship. She talks as if—when you've lost one man, you ought to go to Molyneux for a new outfit and possibly try a new hair-do, and then get another man —just like that. She doesn't say so in so many words, of course, but that's what she damned well means. She's not really much better than all these village sluts round here who've been going with Americans and Italian prisoners while their husbands have been away. Only, of course, with Ann—it's all respectable—sensible respectable biology. One man gone, find another. Stud-farm stuff. When she doesn't make me angry, she makes me feel sick. Oh—damn!"

She ought to have laughed then—and Alan waited for it—but she didn't. She stared angrily at the window. There didn't seem anything for him to say. He made a vague move.

"Yes," she said, getting up, "tea now. Mother hates it if we're late. She's getting awfully fussy about little things."

"Perhaps she doesn't know they are little things," Alan said, very casually.

"No, I suppose she doesn't. The point is—really—that she clings like mad now to the day's routine—you know. It's when you break that in any way, she fusses—and sometimes really loses her temper. We've had one or two nasty rows lately, though I've done my best not to. Come on, Alan. Never mind about those things."

The room might be only the old nursery, which was looking even more worse for wear than Alan remembered it looking before, but Lady Strete had all the silver things in front of her, spirit lamp and all, and was undoubtedly "presiding" at the tea table. Although there were only her three children and her daughter-in-law there, she had put on, like a tea gown, a delicate company air, and even distributed among them artificial little company smiles.

"Your Uncle Rodney won't be down," she said. "Have you seen him yet, Alan? Oh well, you had better look in on him after tea. He never takes tea, of course—just a whisky-and-soda, though he can't always get whisky—even though those London wine merchants of his try to do their best for him. You'll find him just the same, Alan."

"But it's the gramophone now, isn't it? That's distinctly new. I never even knew he liked music."

"Oh yes, darling—he's always been fond of music—in his own peculiar way."

Gerald and Ann exchanged a grin—it was almost exactly the same grin too, although Gerald's large weatherbeaten mug looked very different from his wife's smooth handsome face. Then Gerald winked at Alan. "Had a row with the vicar about music, didn't he?"

"Yes, dear, he did, although I never quite understood what it was all about."

"How is the vicar these days?" asked Alan.

"He's barmy," replied Ann quickly.

"No, dear, that's not quite fair," said Lady Strete. "Mr. Talgarth is quite peculiar now—definitely peculiar. You know, Alan, he lost his wife at the beginning of the war—I think she really kept him going—and of course he missed her dreadfully, and since then he's been distinctly odd. Nobody looks after him properly—I believe the vicarage is just filthy, though nobody goes now and so one just doesn't know how filthy it is—and poor Mr. Talgarth himself is all neglected and queer——"

"He smells now," said Diana. "Honestly he does, Mother."

"Yes. I'm afraid he does, darling. Of course, he's old—and he always was rather eccentric. He doesn't bother at all about the parish now—won't visit anybody and doesn't come out for days on end—and believes all sorts of terrible things are going to happen—something to do with the *Book of Revelation*, which I must say always seemed to me just silliness—all those beasts with horns

17

and things. I've been going over to Crowfield when we could spare the petrol. The only trouble there is that I have to meet the Southams."

"Hello, what's the matter with the Southams?" asked Alan.

"Oh, don't let's start on the Southams," cried Diana.

"No, darling, I don't want to, but naturally Alan wants to know what's been happening. Though you never liked Colonel Southam much, did you?"

"Not a lot," Alan said. He had not thought about old Southam for a long time, but now had a sudden vision of his square leathery face and little bloodshot eyes and could hear again his queer voice, which was at once hoarse and cold. "A sadistic old party, I always thought him. Let's see, Maurice was killed, wasn't he?"

"Don't begin calling the roll, old boy," Gerald muttered.

"Yes, poor Maurice was killed," said Lady Strete, looking gentle and melancholy all of a sudden. "Such a pity, for I always liked Maurice—and never liked his father—or Betty, who's gone and married some poor wretch in the Navy, who's out in the Far East somewhere, and she behaves, I'm told, as if he didn't exist——"

"She was quite tight, last week at the Rollinson's," said Ann in her bright determined way. "Unless she was putting on an act."

"Betty always did put on acts," Alan said, remembering a good deal about Betty Southam, who had been both wild and lovely at a time when he had been easy to enslave and to madden. Well, that was out.

"Colonel Southam got himself elected chairman of the Joint War Memorial Committee," Lady Strete began.

"Not all that again, please, Mother," said Diana.

Lady Strete gave her a quick hard look, then changed it to one of indulgent sympathy. Diana caught both

18

looks and stared down at her cup. Her mother raised her eyebrows at Gerald before turning to Alan. " Remind me to tell you all about it, Alan, sometime when we're alone and not boring Diana."

" Mother ! " began Diana, starting up. But she did not continue the protest. She walked straight out of the room.

" See what I mean, old boy," whispered Gerald. " On edge all the time, poor girl." But then Ann nudged him and he said no more.

" I must say that although that's a horrible suit they've given you, Alan, you do look much nicer in it—just because of the colour, of course—than in that horrid khaki. You look very handsome, darling. Doesn't he, Ann? "

Ann gave him one of those coldly swift, appraising looks that women generally keep for each other, and declared without a smile that he did look very handsome. Gerald, she added, also without a smile, was much too fat these days. He would have to do something about it soon.

" All right," said Gerald, who had one of his surprisingly perceptive moments, " only don't talk as if you're at a cattle show—or I'll put some more on instead of taking it off. Well, I must be going. Promised to ring up a fella."

" And I must have a look at the children," said Ann, getting up. " Oh—what about Darrald? When do we go? "

" We dine there on Friday, dear. I had a telephone message from some secretary of Lord Darrald's this afternoon."

" Friday then—good ! " replied Ann in her brisk way. " Come along, Gerald."

" And you're included, Alan," said his mother. " Diana

absolutely refuses to go, but I was specially asked to bring you. It's the man who's bought Harnworth—Lord Darrald—I forget what he was called before, but you'll have heard of him, dear, because he owns factories and newspapers and things. He has people down every week-end—he's in town during the week—and gives large dinner-parties. You won't have to dress, though, because he comes down on Friday evening himself and doesn't bother changing. I think you might enjoy it. And another thing, darling." And now she lowered her voice, although they were alone. " You can't possibly want to go back to that ridiculous estate office——"

" No, I don't. I was only passing the time there—until the war came down on us. Though God knows what I'm going to do ! "

" Yes, well, Lord Darrald's the very person you ought to meet as soon as possible. He's immensely wealthy and influential—and though rather common, of course, he seems to want to be friendly to the people who matter in the county——"

" Mother ! " And Alan laughed.

" What's the matter, dear? "

" You're just putting it on. You've been reading some old novel. People had stopped talking like that even before the war. Now, come off it ! Do you want me to ask him for a job? "

" No, of course not. Don't be silly. But I thought if you made a good impression—and I know you can if you want to, though you don't always try—well—then ——" And her voice climbed a dwindling trail to mysterious remote heights of wealth and power. She smiled at him. " I'm re-reading Trollope. He's a great comfort, you know. There you are—snug in Barsetshire —and you haven't to worry about Poles and Russians and Chinese and what's going to happen next. Would you like some bridge after dinner? "

" I've almost forgotten how to play—and I never was any good at it."

" You'll soon pick it up again, and it would be nice. Make a four. Did you come back with any of the local boys? "

" Yes, two of the old lot. Good chaps. Herbert Kenford—his father has a farm over at Crowfield."

Lady Strete thought hard. " I think we bought a turkey from them once—I believe Kenford was the name. And who was the other? "

" Chap called Eddie Mold. Lives at Crowfield too. Used to work in the quarry. Strong as a bull and about as many wits—but a grand chap in his way. I must have a talk to them both in a day or two—to compare notes——"

" Notes about what, darling? "

" About—all this——" he gave a humorously wide sweep. " What we think of you people."

" Don't talk nonsense, Alan. I'm not *you people*—I'm your mother. Besides, it's absurd, the way you're talking. As if you were visiting a foreign country or something. When all you're doing is coming back home—taking up your real life again where you dropped it——"

Alan shook his head. " I don't think it's like that, you know. Life's not a walking-stick or something—that you can drop or pick up. My life's been going on—inside me——"

" You know what I mean, dear——"

" Yes, but I don't think it's like that. Never mind. Let's leave it, I think I'll go up and see Uncle Rodney."

" Yes, do, Alan. He'll probably be playing his gramophone records but he won't mind being interrupted, if it's you. And remember, please, darling, he's getting rather old now—he's years older than I am, of course—

21

and he's beginning to show his age in lots of little ways—and sometimes he's——"

He held up a hand. "It's all right, Mother. I won't annoy the old boy. Besides, we always got on pretty well together. I'm looking forward to seeing him again—really."

She smiled. "You go and talk to him then. Cheer him up."

But he could not help turning at the door. "I'll tell you one thing, Mother. Just one of those notes. There's a surprising lot of everybody warning everybody about everybody round here. Rather frightening."

"Alan—why do you say that——?"

"No, some other time. Uncle Rod, first."

It was queer up there on the landing outside his uncle's room. He could hear the gramophone inside and so he waited, leaning against the oak chest of drawers that had always been there, and staring at a large old watercolour of an incredible street scene in some Mediterranean port. The window, further along the landing, was bright with racing clouds and blue air ; but here in the corner there was a warm dusk, the day already dying. But what made it so queer was the music coming from Uncle Rodney's room. A woman—a deep throbbing contralto—was crying farewell to the earth. The strings thinly soared, broke, and fled. There was a faint sweet jangling of harps. The soft silver hammering of a celesta, scattered in the deepening silences, was like some dawn, far-off, pearly, indifferent to men in its pure beauty, stealing over a scene of ruined hearths and dead cities. "Ewig!" cried the woman softly, out of a lost Vienna. The last instruments murmured and died. The silences grew. "Ewig, ewig!" The blue brightens ; the earth awakes in Spring ; but the last whispering farewell is heard no more, because man has gone to find his far long-lost home . . .

"Steady, boys, steady," Alan muttered, more moved than he cared to admit even to himself. And then went in.

His uncle, wearing an old shooting jacket and tweed trousers, was attending, with the huge deliberation of the run-down elderly, to the needs of a gramophone whose giant horn dominated the room. The windows were closed, and the air was sweet and thick with the smoke of Egyptian cigarettes.

"Hello, Uncle. I waited until it was over. Last movement of Mahler's *Lied von der Erde*, eh? And rather clever of me to recognise it after all this time."

"I'm glad to see you, my boy," said Uncle Rodney, shaking hands. He was still impressive, but a vast ruined figure of a man now. "Good God, what have they done to you? It's that suit. Makes you look like a little insurance tout. Where did you get it? The dam' thing's cut all wrong. Sit down."

"Utility suit. Provided for members of His Majesty's Forces on demobilisation."

Uncle Rodney lit another of his fat Egyptian cigarettes, and promptly suggested a distinguished, world-weary diplomat of the 'Eighties. "Give the thing away. Then, the next time you're up in town, you could pop round and see my fella—if he's still there. Can't tell you if he is or not, because I haven't had any new clothes made since this war began and don't propose to have any. Got a pretty good wardrobe, y'know, Alan—it'll last longer than I shall. Got used to that idea now, but at one time it gave me the creeps—that a fella's waistcoats and boots, hairbrushes and razors, all easily outlast him. Got used to the idea—but still feel there's something wrong somewhere." He looked hard at Alan. "Had a rough time out there, eh, my boy?"

" Some of it. Not many of the chaps from round here will be coming back."

" Hm—sorry. You're a good lad, Alan. Wish I could do something for you, but I can't—no money, no influence, no anything. Like the gramophone? "

" Yes, but I didn't know you did."

" No? New idea. Sold my coins a few years ago. Then sold my stamps—good price too. Couldn't decide what to collect—so thought I'd listen to some music. Very good instrument too—this—best there is."

Alan agreed that it was. " And what about Mahler? "

" Oh, this Song of the Earth thing. Thought it too fancy—and too dam' Chinese—at first, but now I'm beginning to understand it. Heart-breaking stuff, really." Uncle Rodney leaned back, produced one of his finest smoke-rings, and eyed it complacently. " Like it now."

" Diana says——" Alan began.

" No, no, my boy, I don't want to hear what Diana says. The girl's all tied into knots because her husband's been killed. Understandable, of course, though he seemed to me a dreary fella. But come to me if you want to know what I'm up to. Don't listen to Diana—or your mother. As for Gerald and that wife of his, they don't know what a man like me feels about things. They don't know any better than a couple of garage hands. That's why they'll be all right. They *are* a couple of garage hands, in a world that'll soon be nothing but a factory, a garage and an aerodrome. The fact is, my boy, the real world—the one worth living in—is finished. These fellas —Mahler, Elgar, Delius, and the rest of 'em—knew it years ago. They saw it all coming, and before it was too late, they looked about 'em, saw what was gracious and charming and beautiful and knew it was all finished. Have a whisky ? I've still got a bottle or two."

" No, thanks, Uncle. But let me give you one, while

24

you go on talking."

"All right, thank you, my boy. Not too much now. It's as if you're in love with a woman—or have been in love with her," said Uncle Rodney, who was known to have been in love with several beauties in his time. "She's a lovely woman—a delicious creature, all delicacy and fire, which is how they ought to be—so don't get yourself tied up to one of these great lolloping land girls. Well, you go and see her—and there she is—beautiful as ever— but then you notice this and that, and suddenly you realise she hasn't long to live—she's doomed. And then —by God—you go away—and you sing it, you make the fiddles cry it out, you set the trumpets sounding it—your old ecstasy, your love, your despair. That's what these fellas felt—that's what I feel—not just about women, of course—though they come into it, naturally—but about everything, about the whole damned drivelling world." Uncle Rodney was quite excited now ; the distinguished diplomat had vanished ; he was no longer even the coun- try gentleman who collected things, a part he had played successfully since 1938 ; but now he was a weird kind of clubman prophet, a Pall-Mall-and-Ritz Jeremiah ; and he pointed a huge shaking forefinger at Alan. "You must be nearly fifty years younger than I am, my boy, and let me tell you, quite plainly, I don't envy you. On the contrary, I'm sorry for you—especially as you're a sensi- tive, quick-witted sort of fella, not like this race of bloody mechanics and chauffeurs we're breeding now. Yes, I'm sorry for you. You'll get up, take your bath, brush your teeth, shave, and put on your clothes—for what? To go and drudge in some hell-hole of an office or factory so that you can come home to some numbered cubbyhole at night, gobble some mess out of tins, and either go to the moving pictures to see how pins are made or sit listening to some government bully on the wireless telling you to hurry up and fill in *Form Nine-thousand-and-thirty-eight*. Once a year you and your wife, who'll be as plain as a suet pudding, and all your brats, who'll have been vaccinated against everything but stupidity and dreariness, will be given a ticket to a holiday camp, along with five thousand other clerks and mechanics and their women and kids, and there you'll have physical drill, stew and rice pudding, round games, and evening talks on tropical diseases and aeroplane engines. And I'll be dead—and delighted."

" You know," Alan said, " you're in fine form. I don't believe you know what you're talking about, but it's coming out in great style."

Uncle Rodney smiled. " The fact is, my boy, I'm very glad to see you. Haven't been talking to anybody lately, and your arrival has done me good. Not rushing away again, are you ? "

" No. I don't know what I'm going to do yet. Too early to decide. But tell me," Alan continued, " if you think everything worth having is ruined and finished, what on earth have chaps like me been fighting for? "

" No, no, my boy," said Uncle Rodney, wagging his huge white head, " you can't catch me with that one. You fought to keep us out of the hands of the Gestapo and all the Hitler louts, to save us from the whole damned German lunacy. Had to do that. Done it myself if I'd been even thirty years younger. The irony is," he continued, leaning back and preparing to enjoy himself, " that if these Nazis hadn't been so impatient and greedy, if they hadn't thrown their weight about so much and provoked everybody, they'd probably have got all they wanted without so much as dropping one bomb. Mass production and mass meetings ! Leadership talking over the wireless ! Nice little houses for nice little people ! Strength Through Joy ! See Italy or the Norwegian

Fiords for eight pounds! That's what they were offering —and isn't it what the mob wants everywhere?"

"You old devil!" cried Alan. "Sorry—but you know what I mean."

"I take it as a tribute," replied Uncle Rodney complacently. "And the fact remains that the world worth living in is finished—can't be brought back. I can't grumble, for I've had my share. But all you've done, my boy, is to catch a last glimpse of it. That's why I'm so sorry for you. Let's have some more music. How about the Elgar 'Cello Concerto?" He rose ponderously.

Alan regarded him with mixed affection and irritation. "You're like a talking dinosaur."

"Don't be impudent, my lad. And wind this thing up, will you?"

So Alan stood there, winding up the gramophone to play straight through the concerto; and he looked across at his uncle who was taking the Elgar out of the record cabinet, and he noticed how everything about the old man—his cheeks and chins, immense shooting jacket, tweed trousers—now seemed to hang in great loose folds; and in that corner of the room which framed his uncle's stooping figure, there were white bookshelves piled high with gaudy memoirs and old French yellow-backs, and the little William Nicholson still life, and a Sickert of the Dieppe period; and it seemed to him, a moment later, before he had finished his winding, that the scene itself was turning into a picture, painted no doubt about 1903, exhibited originally at the New English, now perhaps hanging in the Tate Gallery. "I've got you into the Tate, Uncle. But the record cabinet's wrong."

Either Uncle Rodney did not hear this or he chose to ignore it. "By the way, be careful of those women downstairs. If you don't look out, they'll probably have you married to some clean-living local wench, probably with hands and feet like a farmer's. Heard 'em discussing it, the other night. They may have a list by now. I'm warning you."

"I told Mother," said Alan lightly, "that everybody here seems to be warning me against everybody else. What's the matter with you all?"

"Disintegration, my boy, sheer disintegration." But then, having announced this with a wave of the hand, Uncle Rodney turned and looked sharply at him. "Anybody say anything about me?"

"Not much. Except that you were playing the gramophone hard. So what about playing it?"

"Certainly," said Uncle Rodney. "But for a young man home from the wars, you look altogether too dam' thoughtful for my fancy. No, no; no more talk: Elgar 'Cello Concerto."

And the music began, but it didn't stop Alan thinking, and what he thought was all wrong, quite unsuitable to the occasion. He was home at last, wasn't he? This was it, wasn't it? The rich dark flood of the Elgar came pouring out, but certain doubts and queries could not be drowned and forgotten. From an ocean of vintage port and regret, lost-home-sickness and Madeira, the tide foamed darkly up the beach; but the trip wires and mines remained. . . .

3

HERBERT KENFORD, the one in the grey suit (and he was still wearing it), the farmer's son, was talking to his mother in the kitchen at Four Elm Farm. It was the morning after his arrival. His mother was busy, of course—she always was—but while she bustled round or bent over the huge old kitchen range, she could talk and listen, and she had insisted on Herbert's staying to keep her company. He was her youngest child and the favourite.

" I'd like to have seen some of them places," she said wistfully. " Your Dad never wanted to get about much, but I've always had a hankering for it." This was true. Somewhere inside this stout matron, not quite buried even yet, was a wondering and adventurous child, hungering for distant travel and marvels of land and sea. " Some of the letters you wrote, Herbert, when you put bits in about what you'd seen, were wonderful—I read 'em over an' over."

" Well, I wish now I'd made 'em longer," said Herbert, who was very fond of his mother. " But it wasn't easy—writing—and they wouldn't let you say much."

She nodded, then smiled at him. " Now you're back, you can tell me about it."

" I feel I ought to be doing something round the place," said Herbert. He was a serious and responsible young man, and had not forgotten what farm work was.

" When you've just come back! No need at all for you to be doing anything yet. Everything's being looked after. As a matter of fact, your Dad an' Arthur have gone to Lambury today—on special business."

" What special business? "

His mother gave him a look, at once bright and mysterious, that he remembered from childhood. The years had not changed it. Europe might be reduced to rags and ashes, and half Asia smouldering, but this look, this tone of voice, going straight back to old Christmases and birthdays, remained unchanged. " You'll probably hear tonight—at supper. Arthur and Phyllis will be here—and so will Phyllis's cousin, Edna—you remember her? "

He frowned, perhaps because she had been too arch

29

about Edna. "Yes, I remember her—but why is she coming here?"

"Well, we all thought you'd like to see her again—she's grown up to be a fine girl." She waited for him to say something, and when he didn't, she hesitated a moment or two, then gave him a quick, anxious glance. "You haven't got mixed up with some girl, have you, Herbert—and not told us anything about it—um?"

"No, of course I haven't. Where could I have got mixed up with any girl? Come off it, Mother!"

"Well—I thought—p'r'aps—one o' these Ats or Waafs——"

"Nothing doing."

"I can't say I'm sorry—what I've seen an' heard about some of 'em," said Mrs. Kenford. "Smoking an' drinking an' swearing an' carrying on. How do they expect to bring up children properly an' run a house nicely if that's how they behave—that's what I want to know."

"Well, for that matter," said Herbert, who liked to be fair, "you can't expect 'em to be nice little quiet girls if you shove 'em into uniform and keep 'em driving lorries and sorting ammunition."

"It's no proper life for a girl," she said with profound distaste. "That's why I'm glad you haven't got mixed up with one of 'em. Of course, Edna's quite different."

"I'll bet she is. Well, anyhow," he continued quickly, sharply, as his mother seemed about to interrupt him, "I've not got mixed up—as you call it—with anybody, and not likely to be." And there came then to his mind, like a figure on a distant lighted stage, a clear little image of that cheeky challenging girl in the pub at Lambury. Doris Morgan. Why did she pick on him? What was the matter with her? He had a sudden and immense desire to have some further talk with that one, to put her firmly in her place, her and her dark eyes and smooth face and yellow scarf. Cheeky little piece! Then and there he made up his mind to look in at the *Crown*, one of these nights, and tell her a few things.

" What are you thinking about? " asked his mother, giving him a shrewd glance. He remembered now that she had always had this knack of guessing that his thoughts had wandered off in some direction she did not like. You had to be careful with her.

" I was wondering about the two chaps I came back with," he explained, not altogether untruthfully, for they came into the picture. " Alan Strete—from Swansford. And Eddie Mold."

" If half of what I've heard about that Mrs. Mold is true," said Mrs. Kenford, " then I'm sorry for him. One of that lot that was in the *Sun* or the *Fleece* an' taking men home an' goodness knows what."

" If that's true then I'm sorry for her too," said Herbert grimly. " Once Moldie gets worked up—well, he tears into it. I once saw him set about a couple of S.S. boys who thought they were tough, until old Eddie set about 'em."

His mother deliberately ignored this. " That Mr. Strete, I thought he'd have been an officer." She sounded as if Alan had not known his place.

" He could have been—over and over again. But he had a fancy for staying with the chaps he knew. That's how I came to stay a corporal for so long. He was my sergeant—and I preferred to stay on with him, so I worked it so I didn't get another stripe."

" I'm surprised, Herbert. I wouldn't have thought he was your sort."

" He was my sort out there all right——"

" You'll find it different here," said his mother, " an' don't think you won't. Eddie Mold—Mr. Strete—neither of 'em's your sort here. Never was, never will be. Make

31

up your mind about that, Herbert."

He nodded, then got up. "Have a look round, I think. Nice day again."

"I wish you'd stay here talking to me, but if you want to go out, I suppose you must. But don't forget, Herbert."

"Forget what?" He waited at the door.

"You're out of the army now—out for good, I hope. And I want to warn you. I dare say you've heard some people saying it's going to be all different here after the war. We used to hear 'em, sometimes on the wireless even, before your Dad had time to switch it off, because he couldn't stand 'em. Well, I had my doubts at the time—all that easy talk—they wouldn't have this again, they wouldn't have that—and now I know it isn't going to be much different to what it was. People will sort themselves out again, you'll see. They're doing it already. It's natural, isn't it? So I just wanted to warn you, that's all."

"I'm not arguing, Mother," he told her. "But why did you want to warn me? Where do I come in?"

She looked at him steadily. "You haven't said much so far, Herbert—but I fancy you've changed a bit. In fact, I'm sure you have. And you're like your Dad in lots of ways—obstinate, once you get an idea in your heads. You haven't got that nose for nothing, you two."

"I didn't know I'd changed. Though it's not surprising, is it, if I have? I mean to say, I'm a few years older, and I've been as far as Africa and back, and seen a lot coming and going, and —well, I've seen things and done things I didn't expect to see and do. But even supposing I have changed, what about it?"

"Now look, Herbert, all I want is for you to settle down nicely and be comfortable and happy."

"Well, that's all I want too," he said, frowning a little.

32

" Though it seems to me to be plenty."

She seemed to be relieved, and a certain strain went from her voice and manner. " That's all right then." She smiled at him. " And if you must go out—restless, just like your father—well, off you go."

Out in the yard, where the morning sun was warm and the air full of promise, Herbert looked about him and sniffed appreciatively. He was farmer enough still to realise, without being told, that Four Elm Farm was doing well. It had a solidly prosperous look. And you could almost hear the good things growing.

Old Charlie, the cowman, who had been working at Four Elm as long as Herbert could remember, now came shambling out into the yard, like some ancient figure of earth. He seemed very old now, and quite small, like a little apple kept too long.

" Looks like good farming round here this morning, Charlie," said Herbert, offering the old chap a cigarette. " Doing well, aren't we? "

" Seems so," Old Charlie mumbled. " We got a great wealth o' cows these days, though we an't got proper pasture for 'em."

" You never stop grumbling, Charlie. And you're doing better than you ever did in your life before. Wages up, eh? "

Old Charlie shook his head. " Wages isn't all. 'Tis what wages brings, Muster 'Erbert—an' that's 'ow I looks at it. Yes, 'tis what wages brings. A man might 'ave a pocketful o' paper an' coins an' be no better off. What's to buy now worth the buying? Answer me that, Muster 'Erbert. Beer's like water—an' the price is tur'ble—tur'ble 'tis. As for a drop o' spirits, 'appen for a cold night—'tis completely out o' the question. Even an ounce o' tobakker be more than two shillings. They gives it you with one 'and, an' takes it away with the other. 'Tis all a kind of smooth robbery, that's all." And he glowered at Herbert and sucked contemptuously at his gums.

"I thought you'd moved up, Charlie."

Charlie made a final decisive sucking noise, and loudly cleared his throat. "We've all moved up. An' anything you might fancy 'as moved up too—or moved out. A kind o' game, that's all, Muster 'Erbert. When I started, long before you was born, I was young Charlie Shuttle, at the tail end o' the percession, as you might say, with me pennies in me 'and, waitin' for me bit o' meat an' then me beer an' baccy. Eh? Yes, that's 'ow 'twas. An' now I'm Old Charlie, still at the tail end o' the percession, with me shillings in me 'and—true enough—but getting no more meat nor beer nor baccy. Nay, not so much. A labourin' man, you might say, Muster 'Erbert, with nothing to call 'is own. You follow the argyment?" he enquired anxiously.

"Yes, go on, Charlie. Or is that all?"

The old man looked round hastily, then moved a step nearer and lowered his voice. "If arrangements 'ad been such as give me a few fields an' beasts of me own—or if 'tis all managed so that I looks on a prospect of a hunderd fields an' a thousand beast, an' I can say 'Charlie, all these is yours as much as these is anybody's'—then you see, Muster 'Erbert, I'd 'ave felt properly moved up—as you call it. 'Twould be no game that, but proper advancement."

"Charlie," cried Herbert, "I never imagined what was going on inside that head of yours."

"Well," said Charlie with some complacency, "these war times 'ave changed many this way an' that—as you'll see, Muster 'Erbert, when you've 'ad time to look about an' notice the neighbours. An' these war times 'ave made me a thinkin' man—yes, a deep thinkin' man."

"I can see that, Charlie. You've been hard at it."

"Later," said Charlie, not without condescension, " an'
as times an' places might allow, I'll take pleasure in tellin'
you more, Muster 'Erbert. Meantime——" and now he
raised his voice again—" wishin' you the very best—by
way of 'ealth an' 'appiness ! "

It was pleasant to walk across the fields, to stare at the
curves of the warm moist earth, at the fresh tender green
everywhere, at the primroses and violets above the shining
ditches, and to hear the birds calling. But he found
himself wanting to tell somebody about Old Charlie.
And who was there to tell? His father and his brother
Arthur would certainly not want to hear their old
cowman's conclusions. His mother would not be interested, and anyhow she rather disliked Old Charlie. Alan
Strete would understand, but then Alan had disappeared
into Swansford Manor and might by this time be totally
immersed in his mysterious life there. (Though Herbert
couldn't help feeling that Alan wouldn't be.) And then
the girl with the yellow scarf, Doris, kept popping up,
and somehow or other, without knowing the reason why,
he wanted to tell her about Old Charlie. The fact that
he kept entertaining this daft notion, after rejecting it
scornfully, made him feel uneasy and rather irritable.
At the same time, there, telling him he was home at last,
were the fields, the budding hedges, the flowers, the birds,
all things well-remembered and yet magical ; and beneath
the level of this uneasiness and irritation, they stirred in
him vague longings and desires without a name ; and to
this uneasiness and irritation was added a strange sense
of loss.

It was on his way back to the farm, down the lane, that
he was overtaken by two people on horseback. The
man stopped and turned, so the woman stopped too.
He recognised them as Colonel Southam and his daughter,
Betty. The girl gave him one sharp curious look, then

clearly dismissed him from any further consideration, stared at nothing and thought about something else. Herbert was anything but vain and he knew there was nothing about him to interest this handsome delicate creature for more than a second ; but still there was a kind of insolence in her manner that annoyed him. And now he was boldly returning her father's hard stare. Colonel Southam still looked compact and trim, in his bloodshot leathery style, but obviously he had aged a good deal. His voice was hoarser than ever.

" Let's see," he was saying, " aren't you young Kenford, who joined the Banfordshires? "

" Yes, I am. Back home now—demobbed."

" Good man ! Thought I'd have a word with your father," the Colonel continued. " Find him in, I suppose? "

" No, he's gone to Lambury today."

" Humph ! Well, you'd better give him a message. Tell him that Captain Spiers-Wood can come on the fifteenth, so we'll have the meeting then—and I'd like your father to take the chair—local farmer an' so on. Got that? "

With a care that was not without irony, Herbert repeated the message.

" That's it," said Colonel Southam. " Better come along yourself too, hadn't you? Care to open your mouth in public? "

" No," replied Herbert.

" Why not? 'Fraid of 'em? "

" No, I don't think so. Might be, of course. But I don't want to start opening my mouth in public until I've something to say——"

Colonel Southam smiled grimly. " Don't worry, Kenford. We can find you plenty to say."

" Yes, but I want to do the finding for myself. And

I've only just come home."

"Quite. But you ask your father. He'll tell you." He turned to his daughter, who was showing signs of impatience. "All right, Betty. Shan't be a minute. And don't pull at her like that." He stared hard at Herbert again. "You're a farmer's son—got a dam' good farm there, too—and you've fought for your country—eh?"

"Done my best," said Herbert. "So what?"

"So what? Dam' silly expression. Yankee films. My daughter uses it. Well, now you've got to make up your mind to see that the country's run properly."

"I'm all for that," said Herbert.

"Lot of dangerous people about, y'know," the Colonel continued. His voice had an edge on it now. "Dam' dangerous ideas too. Look at Europe."

"I have looked at it."

"Yes, and what did you see, eh? Packs of Reds all over the place. Can't have that here, can we?"

"I don't know," Herbert said calmly.

Colonel Southam gave a jump. "How d'you mean you don't know?"

"I mean this," replied Herbert, who had made up his mind a few moments earlier that he did not propose to conciliate Colonel Southam. "A lot of places I've been in, the people you call Reds took over because they were the people who'd been against the Nazis all the time—see? And the other sort of people, who were frightened of the Reds, had been collaborating with the Nazis—so they were out. That's how it was over there. What it's like over here—well, I can't say, because I don't know, having just come back."

"The Nazis don't come into it," the Colonel shouted. "They're done with. We've got to think about this country now. And if some of you young fellas don't stir yourselves, this country'll be taken over by bureaucrats, long-haired cranks, and the riff-raff of the industrial towns. And sooner or later, they'll take this farm from under your nose—if you don't look out. Talk to your father. He understands these things. And see you give him my message about the meeting."

Here to Herbert's astonishment, the girl burst out laughing. Her father glared at her. "Come along, come along," he shouted, moving off without another glance at Herbert. The girl was still laughing as they went, and now there seemed to Herbert something disturbing about this laughter. It had no sense in it. It was almost lunatic. Even worse than the Colonel's sudden, face-darkening, voice-rasping rage. As he watched them go, he wondered what was the matter with them.

It was not until evening, just before they sat down to supper, that he could give his father the message from Colonel Southam. His brother Arthur was there too, while Arthur's wife, Phyllis, and her cousin, Edna, were helping in the kitchen. There was an immense party air about the evening. Herbert knew at once that his father and Arthur shared some tremendous secret that would be divulged to him at the proper time and not before. Arthur, who had put on weight this last year or two so that his great red neck looked as if it would burst his collar, was all grins and large sly winks. His father, a tall bony elder, whose usual expression was marked by a gloomy wariness, had tonight a kind of arch look that fitted him even worse than the suit he was wearing, put on specially for the visit to Lambury. This look reminded Herbert of the days when his father had been superintendent of the Sunday School and had done his best, on Whit Mondays, to appear playful and jovial. Mr. Kenford was a devout Wesleyan Methodist of the old school, and regarded with disapproval or dark suspicion almost all human activities except the routine of farm work, buying and selling, making money, saving money, expressing moral indignation, and eating. Thus, he was now out of character, and looked it. Herbert could not help feeling irritated by both his father and Arthur, but at the same time he felt rather ashamed of himself for not entering more generously into what was obviously the spirit of the evening—*his* evening, as he well knew— and he tried his best not to show his feelings.

It was clearly a relief to all three of them, however, when the flushed face of Phyllis looked round the corner, to announce supper. There was more food on the table than Herbert had seen for a long time. The table in the dining-room seemed to have enough food on it for a platoon. There was a whole ham as well as a loin of pork, and these were only the beginning. It was as if the whole fatness and richness of the land had been gathered and then dumped into that room. Wars, revolutions, famines, all were banished. The three women too, shining and triumphant, seemed to have the same fatness and richness. Edna was younger than Phyllis, and was still a girl and no matron, but even she looked almost massive, a solid weight of female flesh, a rich harvest of pink-and-white girlhood, a huge extra course of jam pudding and cream. She was quite a good-looking girl, who kept peeping at Herbert out of her clear blue eyes in the friendliest fashion, even admiringly too, and he liked her well enough. But tonight he couldn't fancy her at all just as he really couldn't fancy all this supper. There was too much of it, and too much of her, for his taste.

" Ah, this is something like," cried his father, looking first at the table and then at Herbert. " And look there." He pointed to some bottles of beer and cider. " You lads know very well I never touch it—never have and never will do—but your mother said you ought to have a drop

39

tonight—so there it is."

"Good enough!" said Arthur, grinning. "but we'll have to watch Phyllis with that cider—I don't know about Edna."

"Go on, Arthur!" Phyllis said, with her fat sleepy smile. "It's not me who'll have to be watched. Nor Edna."

"Well, we don't want all this food just to be watched," cried Mrs. Kenford. "You start carving at your end, Dad. You sit there next to Edna, Herbert. And I'm sure I don't know what I'd have done without her."

Herbert felt he was being helped to pork, ham and Edna. But it wasn't her fault, poor girl, and he answered her shy questions readily enough, telling her where he had been and something of what he had seen. But it was no use trying to make it real to her. You just couldn't get it into this room.

"Mind you, Herbert," said Phyllis, rather defiantly, "Arthur may have just stayed here, helping your father to keep the farm going, but it's been no joke for him— what with all the extra work and Home Guard and all. Has it, Arthur?"

Arthur said it hadn't, and, as something seemed to be expected from him, Herbert made haste to add that he never imagined it had been a joke. "But why mention it, Phyllis?"

"Oh, I just thought——" she began, then hesitated. "Well, I thought you were looking sideways at us once or twice, that's all."

"Then you thought wrong," said Herbert, smiling. He had forgotten how quick women were at guessing your unspoken thoughts and catching your mood. He had spent too much time lately among men. Probably all three women knew quite well he was not at ease, no matter how much he tried to appear to be.

40

"Farm work," said his father, looking up from his enormous plateful, for like many tall bony men, who do not look it, he was a tremendous wolfish eater, "farm work is hard work, if it's done properly. As it's been done here. And we couldn't have got on with this war without it. They've realised that at last. And we'll see they go on realising it. No more monkey tricks with agriculture in this country."

"That's right," said Arthur. "This country's got to keep its food production up, and the folks in the towns will have to pay a decent price for it."

"Any sensible government's going to insist on that," said his father.

"Don't let's have any politics tonight," said Mrs. Kenford quickly.

"I agree," cried Phyllis. "Argue, argue, argue! It's terrible. You ought to hear Sidney. Eh, Edna?"

"Sidney's awful. I told him to shut up, the other night. I was sorry afterwards—y'know—taking him up sharp—but really—the way he goes on!" And Edna looked at the other two women, who nodded and smiled.

But Mr. Kenford, who was an obstinate man, had not quite finished. "Everybody knows my politics. No need to argue about 'em. All I'm saying is that this country being in the situation it is, any sensible government that knows what it's doing is bound to back agriculture. Must do."

"Every time. And if these folk in the towns," said Arthur, who appeared to dislike them, "try to think different, then there'll be trouble, that's all."

"What kind of trouble?" Herbert asked.

Arthur gave him a look. It was an unexpected look, almost startling, because it might have come from a suspicious stranger. Then it vanished, and Arthur grinned. "Never you mind, Herbert boy. You tuck in an' enjoy yourself. You're home now." He looked round for approval. He received it.

So Herbert tucked in and tried to enjoy himself. But he still felt uncomfortable, and strangely sad too. They were all solidly there, putting away the stupendous grub and almost sweating over it, whereas he, a member of the family, one of them, not pretending to be any better than they were, or any different from them, was somehow not quite there. It was as if part of him was in some lonely mid-air. His mother guessed it too, and occasionally gave him a curious look, half-defiant, half-appealing.

Making an effort, he did what he had done the night before, asked questions about the local people they all knew. What had become of this one and that? This worked all right. His father and Arthur gave him all the answers about farms and jobs, and the women delightedly produced all the births, marriages and deaths for him to inspect. And this brought them through the pudding and cream, cake and cheese, until nobody could eat any more and they were all thoroughly stuffed. The beer and cider were passed round, except to Mr. Kenford, who accepted some strong tea and at the same time said that he hoped the rest of them would not regret their " indulgence," as he called it.

" We'll stay in here, Dad, eh? " said Mrs. Kenford. " Then we can wash up afterwards while you men talk things over."

" Just as you like, Mother," said Dad, rather grave now and self-important. " I'll just get the papers."

Herbert had no idea what was coming, but obviously this was the great moment, for which the early part of the evening, and possibly all that day, had been a mere preparation.

" Do you think I ought to stay? " asked Edna nervously.

" Yes, of course, Edna," replied Mrs. Kenford, smiling

42

at her. " It's not as if you're a stranger. We think of you as one of the family."

Oh, they did, did they? Of course this was Phyllis's cousin, Herbert reminded himself. But still, Phyllis had lots of cousins probably, aunts and uncles too—and, for that matter, a father and a mother. Why was Edna then suddenly adopted? He did not like the sound of this at all. He turned and found her glancing at him shyly and sweetly, and felt a fool and a lout when something in the look he gave her obviously wiped out that shy sweetness and produced something like dismay.

" You don't mind, do you, Herbert? " she whispered, leaning towards him, pink and blooming and excited, so that for a moment he wanted to grab hold of her.

" No, of course I don't. Anyhow, I don't know what it's all about," he told her, rather sharply too ; annoyed because she had this effect upon him.

His father was now pushing away the plates in front of him to make room for a large, legal-looking envelope, which he handled with reverence. This was it, evidently.

" Herbert," he began, as if calling them all to attention, " we're glad to see you here, back home at last."

" I should think so," cried his mother.

"You've done your duty," his father continued, ignoring this interruption, " and we've done ours. Nothing to be ashamed of, and perhaps plenty to be proud of. Now you must have been wondering why I didn't have a serious talk with you last night—eh?——"

" Well, no," Herbert began.

But once Mr. Kenford got going, he liked to make a good set speech. " Yes, and I didn't like to explain because I might have spoilt it. You see, I had a bit o' business to finish off today first. That's why Arthur and I went into Lambury. Well, we did our business all right—in fact, we did even better than we thought. And this makes a great difference to you, Herbert. You must have been wondering what the future had in store for you, with both Arthur and you here at Four Elm. Well, you know Joe Ellerby's farm, between here and Swansford?"

"Of course I do," said Herbert. "How is old Joe?"

"Joe's finished. Had a stroke. And anyhow he couldn't carry corn, Joe couldn't. But today I've bought that farm, with everything on it. And Arthur's moving in there, as soon as we can take it over——"

"Arthur, you never told me," cried his wife.

Arthur grinned. "Under orders not to tell. Fine place too, properly looked after."

"I'm talking to Herbert now," said Mr. Kenford, rather severely. "You two can talk about Ellerby's place later. But you see what this means, Herbert? Arthur goes over there. You stay here—and of course I'll be here, though I'll have to give Arthur a hand too—but sooner or later, this'll be yours. And don't forget there isn't a better farm anywhere round here. So there you are."

They all looked expectantly at him. There was kindness in their eyes. They had been thinking about him, planning for him. Moved by this thought, he now felt ashamed of himself. It was not the farm; he could not think yet in terms of work, property, money; what moved him was their concern for his future, which he had not expected—except perhaps from his mother—and which he felt obscurely he had not deserved, simply because he had come back to them almost like some cold and suspicious stranger. Now, following this shame, came a sense of release. His eyes smarted. Here he was, at last, with his own people.

"Well, Dad, that's wonderful," he stammered. "I didn't expect—anything like this. . . . I hadn't thought about it really. . . . I'm very grateful . . . ."

His mother flashed round the table a triumphant glance. " You see ! " it cried.

" I'd no idea you'd be able to buy another farm," Herbert continued, " especially one as big as Ellerby's. You must have done very well."

" We haven't done so badly," said Arthur, with some complacency.

His father took the lead again. " We've nothing to complain of at all. A good property here—and now another one, when it's properly worked up. Whatever silly nonsense they try in this country, a man with a good farm of his own is going to be all right. We can live—and live well—while some of 'em are looking starvation in the face and beginning to come to their senses. And, don't make any mistake, that's the way to see it. A man's got to look after himself—and his own. We're in a better position than anybody else. And why? " Mr. Kenford looked round the table, not so much expecting an answer as defying them to interrupt him. " Imported food might be cheaper than what we can sell ours for, but it's got to be paid for, hasn't it? And we're not going to find it as easy to pay for it as we did. That's certain. Let 'em try it and they'll soon see. And we can produce most of what's wanted and get a fair price for it too."

" You'll be surprised, Herbert," said Arthur, with his fat grin, " when we tell you a few things. Not like it was when you joined up. Oh no ! "

" A lot of these chaps you came back with, Herbert," said his father, " think they're going to ask for this and that—fancy houses, nice easy jobs, plenty of holidays with pay, and so forth—and get 'em served on a plate. But in a few years some of 'em'll be asking where they can emigrate to, never mind whether they get fancy houses and nice easy jobs at the other end or not. When we start facing facts, all this silly talk we've heard will look sillier still. But you've no need to worry, Herbert. We've looked after you just as we've looked after ourselves—couldn't do less, of course, and I'm not claiming any credit for it—and you've got your feet on the ground from now on, and it won't be so long before it's your own ground. Well, that's enough o' that."

It was. It was more than enough. Gone now was that sense of release, that feeling of being together at last. Herbert stared at them, cold as stone. To say nothing of the living, who had put on their new suits with him, there were at least fifty dead, buried in the desert, in France, in Germany, to whom he felt closer now than he did to these people. Voices came back: " I tell you, chum, after the war it'll be all different." " Don't kid yerself. It'll be just the bloody same." " How about it, Corp? " How about it? Feet on the ground! What ground? The odd grave by the jeep trail, where the earth might suddenly move and out of it come a pointing skeleton finger and glaring eye-sockets.

" What's the matter, Herbert? " his mother asked. " You all right? "

" No—I feel——" and he got up hastily. " I think I'd better go out for a bit."

" Eaten too much, boy," Arthur called. " Haven't the stomach for it perhaps, not yet, eh? "

" No, not the stomach for it yet."

The night was calm, chilly, and immense, with a faint glitter of stars. It had nothing to say to him. No man alone meant anything to, or could endure, those cold spaces. You had to be many men, going somewhere, moving in column towards an objective, silent perhaps but keeping in touch, deeply aware of each other and of what must be done together, to face the night without a shrinking of the heart. And now he was a man alone.

46

Commanding himself to say nothing of what he really felt, to let the evening pass as they wanted it, he went back into the house. . . .

4

EDDIE MOLD, the burly one in the brown suit. Still be-fogged by all the beer he had had the night before, he woke up that morning wondering where he was. He had been in so many places—camps, ships, billets, holes in the ground. Now he remembered that he was in his own bed in his own cottage. Alone too. He thought that over again, for his mind worked slowly and insisted upon turning troublesome thoughts over and over. He had come back to find his cottage empty, and Nellie, his wife, away from home. The telegram he had sent—an idea of the Sergeant's that, for Eddie was no sender of telegrams—he had found lying unopened in its little envelope. There was no message left by Nellie, who could not have known he was coming home so soon. On the other hand, the bits of food, off which he had made some sort of meal, told him that Nellie had not been gone more than a day or two.

Two things had upset him, last night. First, finding the cottage empty and Nellie away like that. It was no home-coming. It was all different from what he had imagined so many times. And the other thing was the photo—an enlargement of the one he had carried round with him—of their baby girl, who had died while he was away. It had been bad enough learning about it out there, but now here, in the empty cottage, where she ought to have been running round, it was even worse, though he did know about it already. Seeing that photo, staring at it, upset him badly. Afterwards he had gone round to see Bert Ross, who used to work with him at the quarry and who was still working there, and they had gone along to the *Fleece*, and had a few pints.

Now it was morning and he had his own breakfast to get ready, which wasn't right, not after a chap had been away so long. The cottage wasn't looking as nice as it had done sometimes, though Nellie had bought a few new bits of things—two vases and a clock, and there was a neat little wireless set he'd never seen before—which must have taken some doing out of the money she'd had. Unless somebody had left her something, for there was a bit of money in Nellie's family, and they'd always thought her a cut above him just a chap at the quarry.

After frying the last rasher of bacon and slice of bread, and making himself a strong pot of tea (no milk though), he stood at the door and had a smoke. It was a fine morning, and the village wasn't looking at all bad. His cottage was one of four just off the far end of the main street. Next week, Bert Ross had said, he would be able to start at the quarry, for Mr. Watson had applied for him, through the Labour Exchange, and it was all right. Eddie decided to go along sometime that day to have a word with Mr. Watson. Meantime, he stood at his door in his new brown suit, which was a very fine suit except that it was a bit too tight for him, had his smoke, and stared down the quiet village street.

Then Mrs. Mogson came out. She lived next door, with her daughter (who worked at the Post Office), and she was a nasty old woman, like a bent, jeering old witch. He hadn't seen her since he came back this time, and didn't want to see her now.

Mrs. Mogson gave him a long sly look, which made him feel uncomfortable at once. " So you're back, eh? "

" That's right, Mrs. Mogson. Got 'ome yesterday,

matter of fact."

" Yes, I 'eard yer. My daughter said you was comin' back. Took that telegram, she did. But you're alone, aren't yer? "

" Yes, the wife must 'ave gone to stay with 'er mother over at Bancester. She often does. My telegram must ' ave come after she left—see? "

" Oh, did it? "

" Must 'ave done," said Eddie, frowning at her.

" Oh—must it? "

" Yes, it must," he retorted, raising his voice.

" No need to shout," said Mrs. Mogson. " I'm not deaf even though some people carry on as though they thought I was. I can 'ear all right. I 'ear plenty."

He took no notice of this but looked away from her, down the street.

" Well, you're back, an' not before time too."

What was the matter with the silly old geezer? He stared at her, and thought she looked just like scores of old women he had seen in North Africa, Normandy, Holland. All alike really.

" Yes, it's about time some of yer did come back," she continued, " to 'ave a look at Crowfield—an' never mind 'Itler."

" Well, we aren't sorry to be back, Mrs. Mogson."

This made her cackle—the daft old bitch ! What was the matter with her? Doting now? " Given yer a nice suit to come back in too, 'aven't they? Take care yer don't spoil it, young man. Them big shoulders o' yours look like bursting out of it—so be careful. Strapping chap y'are, these days, Eddie Mold. Short-tempered too, I'll be bound. Well, we've seen plenty o'strapping young chaps round 'ere while you was gone—Americans, mostly —an' black, some of 'em."

" So I've 'eard," replied Eddie shortly.

"Well, yer may 'ear a bit more before you're a lot older," said Mrs. Mogson, obviously enjoying herself. "Just keep your ears open, that's all. An' I 'ope you're not feelin' too lonely, all by yerself. 'Spect your wife'll be back soon."

"'Alf a minute." Eddie called her back. "What's the idea? What yer getting at? Nobody's done you any 'arm, 'ave they?"

"Yes," she replied promptly. "Kept me awake at night when I wanted to be asleep. An' my daughter, who's 'ad to go out an' work an' not lie in bed all morning an' then stay out 'alf the night, my daughter 'as been kept awake too."

"What are yer talking about? Who's kept you awake?"

"You find out. An' then 'appen yer won't act so 'igh-an'-mighty. You an' your new suit!" She cackled scornfully, and banged her door at him.

Brooding over this queer talk, Eddie, who was a fairly tidy chap in his own slow way, went in and tidied the place up a little. Then he decided to buy a newspaper, to see what was happening here at home, and on his way into the village he met Fred Roseberry's wife—widow, really—who was out shopping with their youngest kid, a bonny little girl.

This meeting was awkward. He had not known Fred Roseberry very well before the war, but he had seen plenty of him out there. He remembered Fred telling him when this kid was born, and he had been only about ten yards away when a mortar shell had finished poor old Fred. Of course he wanted to have a word or two, sooner or later, with Fred's wife, but he had planned to leave it until later on. And now here she was, a tallish serious sort of woman; pale and dark, not bad-looking; and very neat and nicely-dressed. He remembered she used to work in a grocer's at Lambury, and Fred had said he was very lucky marrying her. Lot of luck Fred had had!

He guessed it was just as awkward for her. She'd heard about him from Fred. And now she didn't know whether to smile or to cry.

" I didn't know you were back, Mr. Mold," she was saying, taking a pull at herself.

" Got back yesterday afternoon," he said, rather gruffly, not looking at her.

The kid said something that Eddie couldn't catch.

" She says you're not a soldier," Mrs. Roseberry explained, smiling a little.

Eddie, who was fond of kids, gave her an enormous wink. " Used to be—but given it up."

Glancing quickly from the child to her mother, he caught a queer pitying look on her face, before she had time to change it, and she knew he had noticed it. Her pale cheeks were suddenly flushed. She had to say something. " You must be glad to be back. How's Mrs. Mold? "

" Well, I don't know," he explained awkwardly. " She didn't know I was coming—so she's away—over at 'er mother's I expect."

There didn't seem to be anything more to say about that. The little girl saw another little girl she knew, pulled herself free, and ran across. Mrs. Roseberry kept an eye on them. " Fred often used to mention you in his letters. You were together, weren't you? "

" That's right. Saw a lot of him out there. We— well, we all liked Fred—and—and sorry about it—yer know——"

" Yes," she said softly. " Sergeant Strete wrote to me. It was a lovely letter."

Eddie clutched at this. " He's a wonderful bloke, Sergeant Strete—comes from that big 'ouse at Swansford,

51

y'know, but wouldn't take a commission—stayed on with the lads. I'd do anything for that bloke. 'Im an' me an' 'Erbert Kenford—yer know, they 'ave that farm —all come back together. 'Erbert Kenford's another good bloke. Quiet—doesn't say much—but one of the best. We come back together yesterday, just the three of us."

"Yes," she said quietly, bitterly. "Just the three of you."

"'Ere, Mrs. Roseberry, I'm sorry—I didn't think—yer know——"

"No, it's quite all right. Dora, come along," she called. Then turned to him again, somehow easier now. "Mr. Mold, I don't want to bother you now, but sometime will you come and tell me about everything out there—about Fred—and everything? Just once. I haven't talked to anybody yet who was with Fred, and I know you were. And it would help me."

"Well, I'm no good at talkin', Mrs. Roseberry. I'm only a rough sort of chap—Sergeant Strete or 'Erbert Kenford, specially the Sarge, would do it better—still, if you want me to."

"Yes, I do. And—and—Mr. Mold—if there's any way I can help you—there might be something—I wish you'd come and ask me. Will you?"

"Certainly I will," he declared, though he could not imagine how she could help him or why he should ever want any help. Still, she meant to be nice and friendly, he could see. He was glad he had seen her now, if only because she took the taste of that poisonous old toad, Mrs. Mogson, out of his mouth. "I've just been talking to that Mrs. Mogson."

"Oh, she's a horrible old woman," cried Mrs. Roseberry. "I hope you didn't——" And then she stopped.

He waited for her to finish.

She coloured again. " I mean, I hope you didn't take any notice of anything she said."

" Not me. She's daft. Well——"

She nodded and smiled, and he walked on. Yes, a nice woman, poor old Fred's wife. You marry one like that and then go and cop a moanin' minnie. Other blokes manage to duck everything and get safely back home, only to come back to wives that were terrible packets of trouble. No sense in it, no justice.

After buying a paper he had a stroll round, feeling peculiar in his brand-new civvy suit. He met several people he knew and had a word with them, but he also saw a good many he didn't know or couldn't remember. The village itself hadn't really changed at all, for it had had no bombing and there had been no recent building. The only signs of the war were various notices left by the American troops. Yet somehow it all seemed strange to him, the whole place. Here he was, where he'd wanted to be for years, and yet so far he didn't feel he was here. Perhaps because Nellie was away. Coming home was all mixed up with Nellie of course, for a chap wanted his wife. He began to wonder whether he hadn't better send her word or try to get over to Bancester. Of course her mother might be very ill.

" 'Ow's it going, Eddie? " asked Tommy Loftus, who had got his ticket from the Artillery in 'Forty-two and was now driving a bus.

" All right, Tommy. Feels a bit funny at first—back in Civvy Street."

" I'll tell you what it is, Eddie. That Civvy Street we all used to talk so much about, this isn't it. Don't make no mistake about that. It isn't 'ere, that Civvy Street."

Eddie couldn't see what he was getting at. Tommy was always a quick, joking sort of chap. " Where is it then, Tommy? "

"Where it always was. In our bloody 'eads." And Tommy laughed, not very happily.

"I don't get you."

"Look, Eddie, I know what you've been saying for a long time—just what I said. 'Just give me my ticket, that's all.' Eh? Right! Well, I got it, didn't I?"

"Yes," said Eddie grimly, "an' if you'd been where I've been since you did, you'd 'ave been saying 'And a bloody good job too.' See?"

"Yes, Eddie, except I couldn't 'ave 'ad my ticket an' also been where you've been, could I? Not logical, that. Work it out, Eddie. But I know what you mean. An' now I'll tell you what *I* mean. I mean, when you get it, when you come back, it isn't what you expected, see? Civvy Street! You wait."

"But then you've got used to it, Tommy."

"That's just the point. I 'aven't," said Tommy earnestly. "An' I've been back two-and-a-half years. All right, I know what you're going to say. It's been wartime, not peacetime again. I'll grant you that, Eddie. Yanks 'ere. 'Alf the women turnin' the place into a bloody great knockin' shop——"

"'Ere, steady on," Eddie growled.

"Steady on nothing!" cried Tommy, who was always ready to speak his mind. "You ought to 'ave seen the way they carried on. If anybody'd told me, I wouldn't 'ave believed 'em. But I saw it with my own eyes. 'Owever, that's not the point. There wasn't any of them games in my 'ouse—I got there first. But the point is, Eddie, you expect something you don't get. Different to what it was before—but of course better. An' it's different all right, but I'll damned if I can see it's any better. Nor likely to be."

"You off on the Bolshie tack, Tommy?"

"Me? Soon I'll be more Bolshie than the Bolshies.

54

All right, Lizzie," he called to the impatient young woman who was the conductor of his bus, " I'll be with you." He jerked a thumb in her direction, and lowered his voice. " Little Lizzie Fat-bum there is off to Canada soon. You'd think she was going there now, the 'urry she's in. But she's got the right idea. Not just Canada. But she's like the rest of us, she wants a bloody change— so she's goin' to look for it. An' you'll want one soon too, Eddie."

" Not me. I've 'ad too many changes. This'll do me."

" You wait ! You don't know yet what you'll want soon. You'll be surprising yourself. So long, Eddie ! "

" So long, Tommy ! " And he watched the bus move down the street. No need to take too much notice of Tommy Loftus, even though he was a smartish chap. Too much bus-driving. Browned-off. All these chaps who did a lot of driving got the same way. Too much gear-changing and sudden braking.

Deciding that he might as well wait for opening time, Eddie hung about the main street, not far from the *Sun*, and had a few words with two or three chaps he knew ; but he began to feel uneasy, heavy, brooding-like, discovered at last that he did not want to go into the *Sun*, and suddenly set off hastily to return to his cottage. Nellie might be there by this time. But she wasn't. And now the sight of the empty cottage had a bad effect upon him. It seemed to jeer at him, the way old Mrs. Mogson had done. He prowled about, upstairs and down, looking into cupboards and drawers, turning things over, peering into corners, as if he'd lost something and didn't even know what it was.

Out at the back was a little shed he had put up himself when they first moved in, the year before the war. He ended up there, striking matches and poking about. A lot of empty bottles in the far corner, and they didn't look like beer bottles. He began pulling them out, and did not stop until he had brought more than a dozen into the daylight. They were all whisky and gin bottles, and some of them had queer names, Yank style. He carted the lot of them indoors and piled them on the table. Just as he had finished, somebody appeared at the open front door.

This time it was Mrs. Mogson's daughter, the one who worked at the Post Office and usually came home to dinner about half-past one. She was a stuck-up, nosy woman, with Old Maid written all over her. And of course she was staring hard both at him and the bottles. Well, let her!

" I think you ought to know, Mr. Mold," she said in her best Post Office voice, " that Mrs. Mold didn't leave until late yesterday morning. Mother saw her go."

" I'll bet she did," Eddie muttered. " Well, what about it? "

Miss Mogson stared at him harder than ever. " Not until *after* the telegram was delivered. In case you thought of making any complaint."

" Who said anything about making any complaint? " he shouted. " You mind your own business."

" The telegram *is* my business. And it was delivered at once, *before* Mrs. Mold left. That's all." And off she went.

He grabbed the nearest bottle, rushed out to the back, and threw it down as hard as he could, smashing it to bits. And he felt no better. He went out, banging the front door, and no longer feeling hungry now, caring nothing about food and drink, he walked for miles, a stumping figure of bewilderment and anger. Sometimes he was all bewilderment, like a man in some teasing dream in which familiar faces and places change their appearance and become quite strange. Sometimes he was all anger, one man against a vast conspiracy. In the end, when work was just finishing, he found himself at the quarry, at which he stared almost wistfully, as if only that huge battered face of rock could be recognised as the face of a friend.

The manager, Mr. Watson, a jumpy oldish man, discovered him there. " Ah, Mold. Glad to see you. Happy to be back, eh? "

" I dunno," Eddie mumbled. " I'm all in a muddle."

Mr. Watson looked surprised. " Really? Well, I suppose we're all in a muddle to a certain extent. However, Mold, you know that it's all right for you to start next week. Plenty of work here—important work too. And we need a good strong chap like you." He dropped his voice. " Future here for you, Mold, if you behave yourself. You know the work—you're still young—and, well, one cr two of our men here aren't as young as they used to be. You understand—humph? "

" Yes," said Eddie bleakly, " I get the idea."

Mr. Watson gave him a sharp look. " Been on the spree? "

" No, I 'aven't." And now Eddie gave him a sharp look too. " 'Ave you? "

" Come, come, come ! " cried Mr. Watson. " That's no way to talk, is it? "

" No, it isn't," Eddie said slowly. " Unless it's said friendly like. But if you're askin' me, then I'm askin' you."

" Now, now, you're forgetting yourself, Mold."

Eddie considered this carefully. " No, I'm not forgettin' meself. Seems to me it's other people who's been forgettin' me. But I don't mean you, Mr. Watson."

" I should think not," said Mr. Watson. " I put in an application for you weeks and weeks ago, so that you could come back to us as soon as possible. Couldn't do

3

any more, could I? So you can start on Monday."

" Well, I'll see."

" You'll see? What do you mean—you'll see? What is there to see about? I don't understand you, Mold."

Eddie made a huge vague gesture of despair. " Not your fault, Mr. Watson. Don't take no notice of me. Only—I'm 'uman, aren't I? I've got feelings, 'aven't I? I'm a man not a bloody machine——"

" Don't talk to me like that," cried Mr. Watson, shocked. " This isn't the army, you know. I suppose I ought to make allowances—in fact, I am doing—but really, you know, Mold——"

" Look, Mr. Watson," said Eddie earnestly, interrupting him. " I've nothin' against you, an' don't think I 'ave. Quarry's all right too, so far as it goes. So take no notice. I told yer, I'm all in a muddle. I've 'ad nothin' to eat all day," he added, suddenly remembering and feeling empty, " an' I feel all over the blinkin' shop— daft ! So I'd better be off."

Where the road back to Crowfield crossed the main road between Lambury and Bancester, there was a little eating-place, used chiefly by lorry drivers. Here Eddie had a pot of tea and sausages and chips, which he ate in a corner, not noticing anything or anybody : a sullen and formidable figure of a man in a nice new brown suit rather too small for him. It was the same in the public bar of the *Sun* later on, where he took his pints into a corner and brooded there, while the place filled up and soon allowed him to be overlooked in the crowd, the smoke, the noise. But he was able to overhear a few things. There were, for instance, two middle-aged women telling the whole tale not two yards away, and he overheard a good deal, far too much, of what they told each other. At closing time he began pushing his way through to the door.

" Well, look who's here," cried George Fisher, who'd obviously had his share of beer. " If it isn't old Eddie Mold, the famous right back of *Crowfield Rovers*. We're starting the old team again this next season, Eddie. What about it? Or have the old legs had enough? "

" That's right, George," Eddie muttered, trying to free himself. " Too old."

" Go on, Eddie boy. You're looking grand. Isn't he? Just look at old Eddie here."

" Turn it up ! " He made another move to free himself.

" Now, Eddie—just because you're one of our brave boys——"

" Oh—bullshit ! " And Eddie, suddenly losing his temper, gave George a shove that not only sent him reeling back but came near to knocking down half-a-dozen other people.

" 'Ere, come off it ! " " What's the idea? " " Who started that? " They were all shouting and glaring.

Eddie lowered his head and slowly raised his huge fists. He felt like setting about the lot of them. " Anybody want anything? " he demanded. " Cos if they do, they can 'ave it. Well? "

" Outside ! " shouted the landlord.

Eddie told him what he could do with himself, then walked slowly out. But down the road, in the dark, he felt loaded down with misery, hating himself as well as them. All different, and all wrong. And steadily getting worse.

Outside his cottage he waited a minute. The curtains had been drawn but some light was showing. Nellie was back all right. He wasn't drunk but he wasn't quite sober. He was in that half-way condition when sights and sounds seem clearer, more definite, than usual, and when a man appears to notice more. The dark face of the cottage, the streaks of light that promised nothing but more anger and misery, the smell of the ruined little garden, the sad cold breath of the night, he took it all in as he waited.

Nellie wasn't alone. He heard the other voice as he flung open the door. The other woman—to his surprise—was Fred's wife, Mrs. Roseberry, who looked even paler than usual, agitated. Nellie had been crying. Her face was swollen. She looked older, fattish, coarser, and not what he remembered. She started crying again as soon as she saw him.

" Mr. Mold," Mrs. Roseberry began, as if she was going to ask him to do something. But then she didn't know how to go on. He went further in, leaving the door open behind him and making a little gesture towards it. She knew what he meant, half turned to Nellie as if to appeal to her, then thought better of it, and, after a last despairing glance from wife to husband, went out without another word, closing the door.

" Eddie," said Nellie, still crying.

He stood there, looking at her, saying nothing. Something ought to have been there that wasn't there. And then he remembered—the bottles. They'd put them away. He could see them doing it, whispering together and shoving them back into the shed. Must think he was daft. Well, she'd see.

" Eddie." She gave him a quick frightened glance, then looked away and dabbed at her wet face. She looked like somebody else. He hadn't come home to live with this one.

" Don't start telling any bloody lies now," he told her. " Didn't take long to 'ear it all. Proper knockin' shop. And you one of 'em. I 'eard plenty tonight at the *Sun*, and don't want ever to go in there again. Yanks, If they couldn't get it for nothing, then it was a quid for the whites an' two quid for the blacks. Them bloody

60

bottles," he shouted at her. "They told me the tale anyhow—didn't need to 'ear any more. That's what I come back to. And my kid dead——"

"Don't bring her into it," said Nellie, glaring at him. "Leave her out of it. I didn't do anything till she'd gone —an' then I was so miserable, I didn't know what to do——"

"You knew what to do all right," he shouted at her. "An' you went an' did it, didn't yer? Well, go an' bloody well do it somewhere else now."

"Eddie, what do you mean?" She was staring at him with her mouth wide open. Had something done to her teeth too. Probably paid for by what she'd earned on her back.

"What d'yer think I mean. I didn't come back for their bloody leavings. Bugger off!"

"Oh no, no, I can't," she began, wailing.

This only made him angrier. "I've told yer. Outside, sharp! Before I set about yer."

She stood up, angry now rather than frightened. "You won't touch me, Eddie Mold!"

"Touch you!" he repeated quickly. His anger was racing down his arms, quivering in his fingers, rising to his throat and nearly choking him. Then, quite suddenly, he felt sick. "If I do touch you, I'll wring your bloody neck. So don't let me find you 'ere when I come back. I'm tellin' yer."

He went out to the back and there he was sick, all the night's beer returning in a stinking flood. Down his new suit too, some of it. The terrible indignity of life, which the soldier knows better than most men, which he thought he had done with for a time, had him in its grasp again. He shivered above his vomit, then went slowly back into the cottage, his anger gone.

But Nellie had gone too. Perhaps along to Mrs. Rose-berry's. He bolted the door, against Nellie and the whole world. He sat near the empty fireplace, in the old rocking-chair that had been his mother's, and went back carefully and painfully over the scene with Nellie, and then over all that he had heard during the day and all his growing suspicions, and then further back still to the leaves he had had and to the days with Nellie before the war, to the time when they were first married, to the far-off time, as it seemed, before that, when they were walking out, when he would go by bus into Lambury, where she worked then, or meet her at the cross-roads, and they would walk close together through the fields or lie with their arms round each other, Sunday afternoons or on warm windless nights, on top of Quarry Hill. It was as if there were two Nellies: that one, young and fresh and laughing, sweet as the grass, her red-brown eyes sparkling and dancing, her pouting lips telling him he was too strong and fierce and ought to try and behave ; and then this sodden, pudding-faced tart, old before her time, snivelling one minute and screaming the next, with her pick-ups at the *Sun* and her bottles. While this one was somewhere down the street, probably still telling the tale, that other Nellie, the one he had courted and married, had gone and disappeared while he was away. It seemed to him, as he sat there hour after hour, rocking mechanically, that this other Nellie was still existing somewhere, only lost to him. Sometimes it seemed too as if there were two Eddie Molds: the one who had been careless and happy with that Nellie ; and now this one, himself in the chair, cold in the middle of the night, who had come back to find it all different, not a bit what he had thought it would be, not beginning all over again, warm and friendly, and better, much better ; but stale and ugly, full of slurs and jeers, the Mogsons staring at him,

Tommy with his " You'll want a change soon too, Eddie," nasty laughs at the *Sun*, other men's empties and his own vomit in the backyard. . . .

5

IT was Friday evening, about half-past six. Alan Strete and his sister, Diana, had the old nursery to themselves. Everything was happening at once outside : bright shafts of sunlight and slashes of rain, black cloud here and blue sky there, and a rainbow or two ; like a brilliant water-colour of the great period. Inside it was dingy but familiar and cosy. Always when they had talked, Diana had made herself as small as possible, folding and bunch-ing herself in the old leather chair, and Alan had made himself as large as possible, stretched out and sprawling across the lop-sided settee ; and that is how they were now. Alan was smoking a long pipe that had a foul reek and made an irritating bubbling sound. It was all like years ago, which alternately hurt and comforted Diana.

" What's that thing that Uncle Rodney's playing now —I mean when we came down? That frightfully long, monotonous, mournful thing. Did you hear it? "

" Yes. Slow movement of Bruckner's Fourth Sym-phony," replied Alan, who knew about music. " Goes on and on and on. Like most of Bruckner."

" I loathe it. I wish he'd stop playing it."

" You ought to ask him to," Alan said. " He probably would, y'know, Di. He's not so bad really. I've had several good talks with the old boy. He's against every-thing, of course, and is determined to turn himself into a kind of museum piece—but doesn't do anybody any harm. As a matter of fact, I believe he fancies he might

63

pop off at any time."

"Well, I'd hate him to do that," Diana said carefully. "just because he used to be such fun when we were little. But I don't believe it. I believe he'll live years and years —and become more and more peculiar." She waited a moment. "Alan, I wish I liked people more. I'm not talking about Uncle Rodney and relatives now but— well, people in general. If I liked them more—a lot more—it would help tremendously."

Alan guessed why it would but decided that it would be better if she told him. So he asked why.

"Because then I could go and do something with people," she replied. "I want to do something. I can't stick here doing practically nothing. Mother doesn't really want me. And I know there are things I could do. But to do them well, you have to like the people you're working for—and I can't. I've tried and I just can't."

"When and where have you tried?" he asked. He gave the question a rather challenging tone just to make her continue talking.

"Don't be absurd, Alan. I haven't spent the last few years just sitting here doing nothing. I tried the women and children, when I helped with the evacuees. I tried the men, when I worked in the canteen. And I just don't like them. I can't help it. I don't. It's a rotten thing to say, I know—but I can't help it. They seem to me so stupid and messy and ignorant. It didn't matter so much when I had Derek to think about and to come back to, but now, when I haven't, I feel it's hopeless. I simply haven't the patience."

"I don't know about the women and children," said Alan slowly. "But I know the chaps. Lived with 'em for over five years. And of course they are messy and stupid and ignorant. Bound to be. They're bewildered and

baffled a lot of the time. I'll introduce you to my friend
Eddie Mold some time, and if I can get him talking,
you'll see what I mean. But on the other hand these
chaps—and I'm sure it's the same with their women too
—have some very definite virtues of their own, some
wonderful good points that you mightn't notice at first."
He stopped to give her a challenging kind of nod.

" What, for instance? And don't get impatient and
cross, Alan. I'm not being a silly snob. I really want
to know."

He took out his pipe and stared at it for a moment.
" Well," he said, " to begin with, under all the surface
coarseness that probably puts you off, they have a
peculiar sort of—delicacy of feeling—of their own. They
just wouldn't do or say certain things that the people
we know wouldn't hesitate to do or say."

" If you'd seen and heard half the things I've seen and
heard," she began. But then stopped. " Sorry! Go on."

" Somebody—some American, I think—once said
' Power is poison.' Well, these people haven't been
poisoned. I think that's terribly important, Di. It keeps
'em sweet inside. They're never ruthless and they're
never—what shall I say?—insolent, even as somebody
like Mother—to say nothing of the real toughs—can be
ruthless and insolent. You may say they haven't much
opportunity—and of course that's true—but it is a fact
that most of them simply wouldn't even dream of going
out for all they could get. They have an idea of fairness
that goes deep, deep down. Anybody in the army who
had the same sense of fairness, even if he was strict and
drove 'em hard, was all right with them. It's not justice—
that's abstract, an educated man's notion—but this idea
of fairness that moves them. It's something the Germans
don't seem to understand, and that's one reason why our
chaps could never make head-or-tail of the Jerries—and

simply thought them barmy."

"Never mind about the Germans," said Diana. "I'm tired of hearing about them. Of course it's different for you—I mean, about these men. You've been away with them, fighting with them, and naturally you understand their point of view. But, Alan, they all seem to me so stupid—they'll believe anything, they'll say anything—and they don't—don't *try*——"

"They haven't had much of a chance yet, y'know, Di," Alan protested mildly. "They haven't much margin. They have to get a living, to scrape along——"

"Oh, nonsense!" she cried, with a surprising spurt of anger. "I've heard all that before and now I don't believe it. It's the people of our class who haven't much money who do the real careful scraping and managing. These people you're talking about just jolly well let themselves go the minute they have money to spend—drink, football pools, dogs, any rubbishy thing they fancy—and don't look a week ahead. Most of the women we had down here were absolutely feckless."

He grinned.

"I don't think it's funny," she snapped. "And their husbands won't. Unless they're as bad."

"They probably are," he admitted. "But it's when you have property and great possessions that you learn the habit of looking ahead. Often you plan your life instead of living it. And all the religions seem to have been against that sort of thing. You're more of a Christian than I am, Di——"

"I don't think religion comes into this," she said hastily.

"Well, all I was going to say was—that it's these people—who are kind, patient, forgiving, never arrogant, not corrupted by power—who seem to me the Christians. In fact, in some ways they're too Christian. They put

66

up with too much. They don't lose their temper often enough. They grumble but leave it at that.

" Because they don't know any better and don't want to know any better. The women talk about film stars, and the men talk about football. I've heard them. The women down here weren't even interested in the war, although their own men were fighting in it. They hardly ever bothered listening to the news on the wireless——"

" I know," Alan said, " but you've got to understand their point of view and put yourself in their place. The sort of women you're talking about probably don't feel that the news on the wireless is meant for them. The voice is all wrong. The style is all wrong. Without any explanation, it's all about a lot of places and vague military operations they know nothing about. It's as if you suddenly wandered into an advanced lecture on physics. But the men I was with were interested in the war all right. They pretended that all they wanted was to get out of the army—and used to have long silly discussions on how to wangle their ticket, as they called it—but that was all talk. It wasn't what they said but what they did that expressed them. And that's another thing. They rarely talk as we talk——"

He broke off, then scrambled to his feet. " I just saw old Talgarth pass the window. He's come to see us."

" Are you sure? " cried Diana, jumping out of her chair. " He never goes anywhere now—and he wouldn't come here——"

" But I distinctly saw him. Listen! There you are."

" I'm off. You'd better see him, Alan. Nobody else will want to. He's a bit mad—and he smells." She hurried across to the door that led to the back stairs. " Get rid of him somehow," she called as she went.

Mr. Talgarth, who had been the vicar of Swansford ever since Alan could remember, was a very tall man with a long neck, on which his head wobbled curiously. He had always been an odd figure, but now, when he was old, lonely and peculiar, he was fantastic. His hollow unshaven face was framed in long grey hair ; his clothes were torn and stained ; and he had a wild stare. He reminded Alan of a mysterious character—some kind of hermit of Gothic Romance—in a toy theatre he had been given when a child. But Mr. Talgarth's voice had not changed : it was still pleasant, cultured, at once precise and persuasive. And it was now refusing, politely but very firmly, to leave the hall.

"You remember me, of course, sir? " Alan said. So far the old man had shown no sign of recollecting who he was. " I'm Alan Strete."

"Ah, yes. Lady Strete's younger son, of course. Have you been abroad? "

"Yes, sir. With the army."

Mr. Talgarth nodded in his wobbly fashion. And then said, surprisingly : " You were defeated there, eh? "

"Well, at first we were, but not afterwards—of course." And Alan began wondering if he would have to explain the whole final course of the war to him.

"You'll be defeated here," said Mr. Talgarth, and pressed his lips together. " I have been defeated here."

Time and loneliness had certainly defeated him, but clearly that was not what he meant. Alan did not feel there was anything he could say.

"If you have considered these matters," said Mr. Talgarth gently, " you will have noticed that the fourth kingdom in Daniel's first vision has a distinct likeness to the fourth seal in the *Book of Revelation*."

"Is that the one about the pale horse? "

"A pale horse, and his name that sat on him was Death," Mr. Talgarth quoted, without any particular emphasis, " and Hell followed with him. And power was given unto them over the fourth part of the earth, to kill with sword, and with hunger, and with death . . ." He seemed to retire into some constant dream.

Alan waited a moment or two, then felt he ought to say something. "Is it—er—your idea, sir, that this fourth kingdom and fourth seal represent this period?"

Mr. Talgarth opened his eyes very wide. Alan now noticed for the first time that they were neither grey nor yellowy-brown but a curious mixture of both. What was happening on the other side of those eyes?

"Undoubtedly," said Mr. Talgarth.

"And nothing to be done about it?"

"My dear young man," the old vicar began, with a touch of impatience, "I don't expect you to believe in the truly prophetic character of these Biblical passages. That would be too much to expect. You know better of course. Of course, of course! But I happen to have given these matters some earnest thought. Let us forget the Bible for a moment, which I am sure will make you feel much happier." He held up a long and very dirty fore-finger, which had a bitten cracked nail. "We shall of course proceed to destroy each other. That is inevitable because there is no longer anything to bind us together."

Alan muttered something about "common interests."

"Your common interests are worth nothing," replied Mr. Talgarth sharply, tapping Alan's tie with the fore-finger. "What men remember now is what divides them, not what unites them. One group stands in the way of a larger stronger group, and so it is destroyed. But then within this group, divisions occur, more challenges, more destruction. Finally we come to individuals——"

"But this isn't happening," Alan protested.

"Not yet. But it will. The disintegration will inevit-ably continue. We separate ourselves in order, in the end, to destroy ourselves. This separation from each other, which began with the separation from God, is the beginning of Hell. We are, of course, in Hell now," he concluded with an air of finality.

Alan could not think of a fairly polite but also adequate reply to this statement, and so he let it pass. There was silence for a few moments. Mr. Talgarth looked round the hall.

" This house is not as well kept as it used to be " ; he observed, frowning. " Neither is my vicarage. In fact, the vicarage is much neglected—filthy. This isn't filthy, but it isn't what it was. Most of the cottages appear to be badly kept too now."

" It's the war, you know," said Alan.

" The war in the larger sense no doubt—that is, with all that war brings—idleness, irresponsibility, drunkenness and fornication. All inevitable, of course. You might as well try to preach against the rising of the sun or the violence of the South-West wind. Do you know the Bishop? "

No, Alan didn't.

" He's a little political busybody," Mr. Talgarth said sharply. " Sends me appeals and pamphlets and rubbish as if we were a pair of social workers. The man isn't a priest. He should be superintending some charitable institution—some orphanage, old women's home, hostel for decayed governesses. He and I are in Hell, and he doesn't even know it yet. But I'm detaining you."

" No, no, but I was wondering. Do you want to see my mother—or Uncle Rodney? "

" Your Uncle Rodney—certainly not," said Mr. Talgarth, with decision but quite pleasantly. " He was always something of a trifler—if you'll allow me to say so—and lately has been quite eccentric. Came worrying me with some nonsense about music. Your mother of course I am always delighted to see." He looked at

Alan expectantly.

" I wondered if you'd called to see her about something," said Alan.

Mr. Talgarth gave this some thought. " I couldn't have called to see you, delighted as I am to see you, because I didn't know you were at home. Yes, I see your point It must have been your mother I wished to see. Now what was it? Ah yes—the morning services. Here she is too."

Lady Strete was dressed to go out for the evening, and now Alan remembered that she and Ann, Gerald and he were going over to Harnworth to dine with Lord Darrald.

" How d'you do, Mr. Talgarth. What a surprise ! " she cried, then turned to him. " Alan darling, hurry up and change. We're dining out, remember."

" I know.   But I'm not changing."

" You needn't dress.   But you can't possibly wear that dreadful suit."

" I can, Mother.   In fact, I insist on wearing it."

" Darling, don't be absurd.   You know it doesn't fit you properly and it's the wrong shape.   And you must have some decent clothes left somewhere.   Now go and have a look, while I talk to the vicar."

But he didn't have a look. He spent a couple of minutes in the bathroom, and then, to kill time, looked in on Uncle Rodney, who had now finished his Bruckner and was lying on the sofa reading *Pitcher in Paradise*.

" Who's this fella Lord Darrald you're dining with? " asked Uncle Rodney.

" He's bought Harnworth——"

" More fool he ! I wouldn't have that dam' great barracks as a gift.   What else has he bought? "

" He controls the *Daily Gazette*, the *Sunday Sun* and a few other newspapers——"

" Never read 'em.   Industry—and so on? "

"Industry and so on," replied Alan. "Mother says he's immensely wealthy and influential and rather common of course. She's probably taking me along in the hope that his lordship will take a fancy to me and offer me a job."

"He won't take a fancy to you in that insurance tout's suit," Uncle Rodney said.

"Then he won't take a fancy to me," Alan said. "And anyhow perhaps I won't take a fancy to him."

"Quite right. As a matter of fact I believe the only way to get a job out of these fellas is not to care a damn whether they offer you a job or not. So you'll probably get one. But look, my boy, don't become one of these gossip fellas who go lunchin' and dinin' out all the time and write it up."

Alan laughed. "That's all dead and gone."

"Don't you believe it, my boy. You're out of touch. Had a letter only yesterday from Johnny Delmaine, and he said his youngest boy had just been given a contract to do this gossip stuff—fifteen hundred a year and plenty of expenses, Johnny said. So there you are!"

"My God—we're not starting that all over again—surely? I'll ask about it. By the way, old Talgarth is down below. I've been talking to him."

"You can't talk to him," said Uncle Rodney. "Mad as a hatter. Fourth Seal, eh? All that stuff."

"He says we're in Hell here and now. And I must say there have been times lately when I've felt like agreeing with him. He says we'll destroy each other."

"Fiddle-de-dee! Probably breed like rabbits from now on. You'll see. What we'll destroy—in fact, we've practically destroyed it already—is any life really worth living. All factories, malted milk and crooners. You'll travel at four hundred miles an hour from anywhere to anywhere, only there'll be no point in it because it'll be just as dull and idiotic at one end as it is at the other. The Russians and the Americans between 'em will settle what everybody should have. If you don't like the Russian Cement Workers' Annual Conference, then you can try the Jitterbug Contest in Los Angeles or the Garment Trade Operatives' Ankle Competition in New York."

"You could take an Ankle Competition, Uncle Rodney," said Alan grinning.

"Certainly I could," the old gentleman retorted, "if I thought there was some real personality, some feminine grace, fire and devilment, attached to the ankle. But not when all that's been flattened out to one dead level of half-witted tasteless stupidity."

"Now, look here," said Alan, with a touch of seriousness, "do you think I'm duller than you were at my age, and have less character, personality, and all the rest of it?"

"Without a doubt," Uncle Rodney said. "You didn't know me when I was your age, so I can forgive you for even asking the question. You're a nice lad—brave as a lion, no doubt—quite intelligent and so on—but nobody my age would say you'd much colour and fire and personality. Not a bit of it. They'd say—as I'd say—you're a decent, dependable, but dullish fella."

"My hat, they would, would they?" Alan stared indignantly at his uncle. "Look here, you know nothing about me. You don't know what my life's really like. Because I come in here, and listen politely——"

"To my nonsense——"

"Yes, to your nonsense. And it *is* nonsense, y'know, uncle. I could tear it to pieces."

"You haven't done," said his uncle calmly. "And that's significant. No, don't start now. You haven't time anyhow, if you're dining over at Harnworth. Tootle off—and don't forget to tell me tomorrow about this fella Darrald."

No young man of spirit wants to be considered decent, dependable but dullish. Alan went downstairs still resenting that description of himself. Uncle Rodney might be a monstrous old *poseur*, whose opinion didn't matter, but Alan couldn't help feeling ruffled. Dullish indeed!

" You wouldn't call me dullish, would you, Gerald? " he asked, once they were outside the gates. Gerald was driving and Alan was sitting in front with him.

" No, old boy, I wouldn't," said Gerald. " You're one of these odd chaps, I'd say. Always were. Wouldn't take a commission, for instance. And then—wearing that dam' silly suit—got it on now, haven't you? And all that writing you used to do."

" It wasn't any good, that writing."

" Of course it wasn't. Told you so at the time. But you would do it. And soon you'll be tryin' some other fool thing. Perhaps paintin'—or something."

" Decent, dependable and dullish—that was me, Jerry."

" Never heard a rottener description of anybody," Gerald grunted. " You're hardly decent. You're not dependable. And, I repeat, not dullish. They must have meant me, not you, old boy. I'm pretty decent and dependable, and often I'm damned dull. I'd often bore myself if I was easily bored, which I'm not. By the way, Mother thinks you ought to keep on the right side of Darrald."

" Make a good impression? "

" That's it, old boy. With any luck I propose to make a good impression on his food and drink tonight. I'm told he does one very well, which is more than we do ourselves at Swansford these days."

74

" What's that, Gerald? " said his wife, leaning forward.

" Hope Darrald's going to give us a good dinner," Gerald roared.

" That's not what you said."

" Well, it's what I meant. Somebody's been tellin' Alan he's a dull fella."

" Alan certainly isn't," cried Lady Strete. " Are you, darling? I believe Lord Darrald likes amusing people, but I think if I were you, darling, I'd be rather careful tonight. Wait until you know him better."

" Perhaps I shan't want to know him better, Mother," Alan shouted above the noise of the car. " And I don't feel much like being careful tonight."

" I should pack up this conversation, old boy," Gerald muttered. " It's a strain, and not likely to get anybody anywhere. Hello, that's old Southam's car. Probably on his way to Harnworth too. Somebody with him? Taking Betty along, eh? You'd better look out."

" Betty doesn't worry me," said Alan.

" Well, it wouldn't take her long to worry me, old boy. I'll just nip in front of old Southam. Safer for everybody. There we are. Now for Harnworth—and a good short drink or two before dinner, eh? "

The short drinks, which included some excellent pink Bacardi cocktails, were waiting for them in the library, a fine long Eighteenth-Century room, nobly furnished with mahogany and innumerable rows of old calf-bindings. The Strete party arrived before Lord Darrald himself and the people he was bringing down from London for the week-end. This interval gave Alan a chance to talk to Betty Southam, now strangely announced as Mrs. Ilminster.

" Alan, I didn't recognise you at first," she said, smiling her secret daft smile. " I took one look and thought you were merely one of Lord Darrald's drearier secretaries.

Why should I think you look dreary, darling? You're not dreary—never were, never will be. But you've changed your appearance somehow. Why?"

"Army haircut. This suit. What I'm feeling perhaps. Another drink?"

"Yes, please. What about me? How do I strike you?"

"Just the same. Beautiful. A trifle odd. Rather inhuman——"

"The trouble about me is I'm too human. But you're really still telling me the same old things, aren't you? Who was it you used to say I was?"

"Undine. I was very young at the time. We can let that go," Alan said, still staring at her. "But I see what I meant. It's the shape of your face, Betty—and the way your eyes are set—wide apart and rather slanting—and that wicked long mouth, curling up. With the pale mask effect too. And that long neck—a very beautiful neck, Betty. Yes, it's the same old character—the young witch, the sea-maid, the naiad, the gold-and-white fay, the Troll King's daughter——"

"Alan, I realise it now. I've missed you. Nobody talks to me like that any more."

"Nobody ought to, now that you're Mrs. Ilminster. Except of course, Mr. Ilminster. What's he like, Betty?"

"Large, rich and Navy. Commander to you."

"What's he commanding?"

"A destroyer somewhere in the Pacific. You've just come out of the army, haven't you? Are you married or anything?"

"No, nothing."

She winked at him swiftly over the glass she had raised. Betty was only a fairy-tale creature when in repose and preferably at a fair distance. "Good! I thought somebody like Gerald's Ann might have grabbed hold of you. She thinks I'm poison, though Lord knows she can have poor old Gerald for me. I spent months and months near Portsmouth pouring out pink gins for dozens of big hearty chaps just like Gerald. Bob knows them all. But never mind all that. I think this is going to be *fun*."

" What is? " asked Alan warily. " You don't mean this dinner-party? "

" Crikey—no! This'll probably be a stinker. It's a pity we can't just pop off to a pub somewhere and get quietly tight. You could tell me all about myself then. You do it beautifully when you're rather tight, Alan. That's what I've missed—I realise it now—after all these years of hearty chaps."

" Perhaps I'm a hearty chap too now."

" Don't be silly, darling. And let's have another quick one before the introductions and social chat begin."

There was only just time for a quick one, their third ; and they were large strong cocktails. Lord Darrald and his other guests now arrived. He was different from what Alan had vaguely expected ; not at all the coarse, massive, fleshy, red-necked brigand that he had imagined. Darrald was smallish and not very thick-set, with something bleached and dried out about him, and suggested to Alan a powerful ecclesiastic in mufti. He went round carefully shaking hands, and first gave everybody a sharp look, as if inspecting a guard, and then followed it with a slow smile. This smile was the best thing about him. The worst, Alan decided, was his manner of speech, his voice and style. He spoke jerkily, using few words, and had a kind of bogus American accent, as if a not very good English actor were attempting to play a City Editor from Chicago.

Lord Darrald had brought with him four guests, and his secretary, a wary middle-aged man called Newby. There was Mrs. Penterland, who was apparently a famous beauty. She was certainly beautiful in her own fashion, which was large, blonde and very elaborate; and she seemed to Alan much more like an historic handsome building or monument than like a real person. She made you feel she ought to be open to visitors from ten in the morning to dusk on weekdays, two-thirty to dusk on Sundays, with a charge of sixpence for admission and another sixpence for the small handbook. She hardly spoke at all but constantly distributed vague smiles. The other woman was very different. She was thin, dark, mannish, and never stopped talking. Her name was Billie Arran; and neither Alan nor Betty had ever heard of her but both of them guessed they were supposed to know all about her. She gave the impression that she had been everywhere and known everybody. The two male guests were also in sharp contrast. One of them, Sir Thomas Stanford-Rivers, was a Tory politician, pink and bland, smooth as a peppermint cream. At some earlier stage in his successful career he must have decided that his eyes ought to twinkle, and now he kept them twinkling and twinkling. The other man did not twinkle but blinked and twitched. His name was Don Markinch, and he was one of Darrald's managing editors, a high-powered newspaperman of the American type, all nerves and cigarettes, the kind of man who for years had been dropping ash on his food and living on alternate doses of benzedrine and barbiturates. At least, that was the impression he made upon Alan, who wondered how the man would get through the week-end here without a war, a revolution, or a new advertising policy.

But then Alan felt a bit tight. Three unusually strong cocktails on an empty stomach, the sight of Betty again, and this grand party atmosphere, had worked together to make him feel dizzy. He was in the mood when at any moment life would seem either radiant with promise or almost unendurable. The Eighteenth-Century portraits in the dining-room leered at him and acquired a mysterious significance. Newby, the efficient secretary, deftly sorted them out round the dining-table, and Alan found himself sitting between Betty (which was no coincidence) and that galvanised skeleton of Fleet Street, Markinch. An ancient butler, who might have been hired from a repertory company to play the part, and three broad-faced foreign maids served the meal, which was the best Alan had had for several years. He drank claret. Betty drank champagne. Markinch appeared to be dining on Evian, white tablets and cigarettes.

"How do you feel, darling?" asked Betty.

"Bit peculiar," Alan said. "Those two portraits came into it somehow, but I haven't worked it out yet."

"Don't bother," she said. "Tell me about me. That's what you do best, and I need it badly."

"Not now, and not here. Do you think my mother's trying to interest Darrald in me? I saw him give me a look."

"Yes, of course she is."

"Well, she needn't. I'm against it."

"Then you're an idiot. Look at Mrs. Penterland, smiling at nothing. The point is, of course, she's obviously as blind as a bat and won't wear specs."

"Quite right. You might as well put a pair of spectacles on the National Gallery."

Betty giggled. Then Sir Thomas Stanford-Rivers, on the other side, claimed her. There was now nobody for Alan to talk to because Markinch was exchanging rapid remarks with the Arran woman, the pair of them dominating the lower end of the table. It was all of course "inside stuff." Christian names or nicknames for all important personages. London, Washington, Moscow,

Chungking, New York, Paris, Rome—the air age, the global outlook. All miles behind the scenes. It put Alan where he belonged, among the hundreds of millions wistfully looking on and wondering what next. He glanced across at Gerald, who was enjoying it all, food and drink and importance, and looked larger and even more innocent than usual. Good old Gerald! But who the hell were Billie Arran and Markinch that they should know it all? Why not Herbert Kenford and Eddie Mold and that girl in the pub at Lambury, the one from the aircraft factory who tackled Herbert so fiercely, and he himself, Alan Strete—what about them?

Now Markinch turned to him. " Sorry—didn't catch your name? " He had a hoarse weary voice.

" Strete. That's my mother talking to Lord Darrald. And that's my brother. We live near here. Swansford."

" County family, eh? "

" I'm never sure what that means," Alan said, " but I suppose you can call us that."

" I was born in Liverpool," said Markinch, " not far from Scotland Road. Tough slum. Left school at thirteen. And then these belly-aching Labour men say you can't get on in this country unless you come out of the top drawer. Look at me. Bottom drawer."

" I see," said Alan.

" They don't know what they're talking about. Any man—doesn't matter where he comes from—can get to the top in this country if he wants to."

" And is willing to pay the price," said Alan, who didn't see why he should be lectured to by this chap.

" What price? " asked Markinch suspiciously.

" Whatever they're asking for places at the top. I wouldn't know what they are. I'm not at the top. I'm not even halfway up."

" What d'you do? "

"Just come out of the army. So I'm not doing anything yet—except staying late in bed every morning."

Ann leaned forward from the other side of Markinch. "He refused to be anything but a sergeant. And he was in the infantry and fought right through North Africa, Sicily, Normandy—and everything. And he——"

"All right, Ann," he told her, cutting her short but not too roughly, "nobody wants to know."

"You're wrong at that," said Markinch. "I'm interested. Tell you why later." He had to break off because the Arran woman was screaming at him to confirm something she had just said. A moment later the pair of them were again doing their "inside stuff" crosstalk act. "My God, you ought to have heard the P.M. when Moochy took that Washington call." That was the line.

Alan refused the port but accepted some brandy. Betty took some brandy too. "How's it going, Alan?" she muttered.

He leaned a little towards her. "I think it's having the wrong effect on me," he murmured in reply. "I used to be a chummy drinker—as you may remember—but now it seems to be turning me into one of these suspicious and aggressive types."

"That's a pity," she whispered. Her hand stole across and gave his little finger a sharp nip. "When are we going to talk about me?"

"Why this line? In the old days, when I used to talk your head off, you soon got bored."

"Not when it was about me. Beside, I'm different now. Older. Also, I've had years of hearty chaps who can't talk properly. And a girl ought to be talked to—and talked *into* things." She turned that enchanting long neck of hers and regarded him earnestly. "Don't tell me the army's spoilt you, and that now you're just another man of action and few words. Don't tell me that, darling."

"All right I won't. But your father's glowering across at you, Betty. He probably thinks you're tight."

She shot a brilliant smiling glance across the table. Then she whispered : " No, he doesn't. The trouble is, he's rather tight himself. He's never got over Maurice, you know. And he shouldn't drink very much—poor old sweet—because he's got a terribly high blood pressure. The result is, he's always denouncing everything all the time. The least thing starts him off. For instance, we were out riding—yesterday afternoon, I think it was— and he stopped to talk with one of the Kenford boys —a dreary-looking young man with a long face and a big nose—— "

" Herbert Kenford," cried Alan, with that delighted recognition which comes when two worlds suddenly overlap. " We served together. He's a great pal of mine."

" Then you must be going dreary too, darling. We'll have to do something about it. But anyhow, this Kenford boy stood up for himself a bit—it was something about politics, I think—and Daddy instantly flew into a rage. I had to laugh. But it was no joke afterwards, because I had hours of it. He can't help it, what with one thing and another. It's all rather hellish, isn't it? Say it is, Alan."

" All right it is. Look—you're off."

" Oh gosh—this'll be deadly. Don't you chaps stay too long here."

Watching her sail sweetly out with the other women, Alan felt a sudden and inexplicable heartache. He was not in the least in love with her. That had all gone years ago. But at that moment she was still the exquisite image of love, the very shape and colour put on by the old enchantment, and so she seemed to take the bloom of life with her. The men remaining round the table appeared to be so many heavy wooden dummies. Glumly Alan moved up at a signal from his host. He also accepted some more brandy but refused a cigar. Feeling the need for tobacco, however, he lit a pipe.

Lord Darrald gave him his sharp look and then his slow smile. Thinks I'm a cool young card, thought Alan, not much caring what Lord Darrald thought of him. He prepared himself rather sullenly for more " inside stuff", more " off the record " talk, more nicknames for the great, more global " hush-hush," more advance notes on tomorrow's headlines and next Sunday's leading articles. Sir Thomas Stanford-Rivers had crossed over to talk to Colonel Southam and Gerald. Newby had disappeared, as if to whisper discreetly to the ladies. (Alan could imagine him doing it too.) Don Markinch was twitching and coughing at Alan's other ell ow. He was wedged between the great man and one of his chief lieutenants, and would have to take it.

" Say, Don," Lord Darrald jerked out, " this young man—just left the army—in the ranks too. What about it? "

" Just about to tell you, Boss," said Markinch. " Going to talk to him too. It's an angle."

Darrald nodded, then looked over his cigar at Alan. Out came the slow smile. " What about it, Strete? Like to tell us things? Man with your background in the ranks can tell us plenty. Might tell the public too—if it was fit for 'em to hear. Eh, Don? "

" Had the same idea," said Markinch. " Listen, Mr. Strete—what are they thinking, what are they talking about, what are they wanting—these fellows who're coming back now? "

Darrald nodded and smiled again. " Go ahead, young

man. Here's your audience. Could hardly have a better."

Alan still hesitated. They thought he was shy. In a way he was shy, but not in the way they thought. At that moment, to those two, he just didn't want to talk about this subject. They didn't see what he was seeing, didn't feel about it as he did. He had a great desire simply to say something very brief and very rude. But he was a guest ; he would have to make some sort of reply.

" Well, it's not easy, y'know," he began slowly. " If you talked to most of the chaps, you'd find 'em rather apathetic and cynical about things in general—and just glad to be home again. They'd tell you they didn't expect anything very much except no more parades, comfortable living in Civvy Street, the wife and kids or the girl friend again—all that. That's what they'd say. But, you see, they hardly ever say what they're really thinking and feeling. Most of 'em. I don't say all." He stopped and glanced from one to the other. Any questions.

" Go ahead," said Lord Darrald. " We're interested. Only don't make it too long."

" Right, I won't," he replied, with a change of manner. If they wanted it short, they could have it short. And see how they liked it. " Underneath all that, most of these chaps really expect something wonderful to happen, a new sort of life. And when it doesn't happen, the fun will begin."

How Markinch reacted to this, Alan didn't know because he was looking at Lord Darrald, who took it quite calmly. " What kind of fun? " he asked.

" I don't know," said Alan, with a touch of irritation, " and neither does anybody else. They don't know themselves. They hardly know they're expecting anything wonderful. But they are."

" And expect to have it handed 'em on a plate, eh? "
said Markinch.

" Yes, of course," Alan replied. " They've been taught
—or at least encouraged—to expect it that way. *You do
the fighting, boys, we'll do the rest.* That's been the line,
hasn't it, ever since Dunkirk. Well, they've done the
fighting."

" Wait a minute," cried Markinch. " Do these fellows
realise the position this country's in—— ? "

" Hold it, Don," said Lord Darrald, in his best American manner. " Don't need to get started on that. Go on,
Strete."

" Go on? I've finished. I've told you what I feel.'

" You haven't told us anything yet."

" Well then I haven't anything to tell you."

" Boss," said Markinch, who liked to be American too,
" he's holding out on us."

" Seems like it."

" I'll only add this," said Alan rather wearily. " A lot
has been said lately about the end of the last war. I'm
too young to know exactly, but I've gone into the subject
a bit with people who do remember that time, and I've
come to the conclusion that the likeness between the men
of the last war and the men of this is only superficial.
There are real and important differences."

" Such as? " his lordship prompted.

" Once it strikes home to them that they're going to
be disappointed, that their *secret* hopes—and the fact that
they are secret is important—are coming to nothing, then
our chaps won't merely threaten trouble, as the last lot
did in the early 'Twenties, they'll *make* it. Deep-down
they're getting impatient. And they've seen a lot more
in this war than the other lot did in theirs."

" A lot more of what—fighting? "

" No, the world—and what goes on in it. Quislings,

black markets, reactionaries ganging up, people's resistance movements. Often they've learned for themselves who liked the Nazis and who didn't. Quite an education in its way," Alan added.

"That's okay. We don't mind that," said Markinch.

Lord Darrald held up his hand. Then he gave Alan his sharp look but let it remain much longer than before. The slow smile came at last, but Alan had to wait for it. In spite of the good liquor burning inside him, Alan felt young and helpless. At the same time Lord Darrald suddenly seemed immensely formidable, a sort of emperor. There were legions somewhere waiting for his command to move. He was no longer the rich man who had bought Harnworth and wished to know some of the nice people in the county. He was power.

"Listen, Strete, you haven't told us very much," he was saying, "and you're all wrong. These chaps won't make any trouble. Less than last time. It was the trade unions then. But the General Strike called their bluff. Now the unions know better. They're all right. Shan't have any trouble with them. As for these boys of yours expecting something, I know what they want. They want some fun. Don't blame 'em. Something to look forward to. Dog tracks, cheap racing, plenty of football, better movies, good places to eat and drink where they can take their wives, nice holidays. We're campaigning for all that now—eh, Don?"

"Running it hard," said Markinch. "And getting a great response."

"They want more than that stuff, you know," said Alan. And he couldn't help sounding subdued. The confident young fighting-man, telling the old buffer a thing or two, had disappeared.

"Yeah. Steady work and wages," said Lord Darrald calmly. "Houses too, when we can build 'em. But that's all. We know."

Alan had to make an effort. " I'm sorry, but I don't agree. It isn't all. They don't know exactly what they want, but it's more than that—just bread and circuses." To his annoyance, he found his voice trembling.

" Have some more brandy," said Lord Darrald. " It's good stuff. I can vouch for it. Now I'll tell you what you're doing, Strete. And no need to be ashamed of it. We've all done it before we learnt better. You see that these chaps want something—and they don't quite know what. So you begin reading your own mind into theirs. You jump to the conclusion that what they want is what you want."

" You've hit it right on the nose, Boss," cried Markinch.

" We can't afford to do that," Lord Darrald continued. " We sell newspapers. So we daren't kid ourselves. Now here are some facts. The *Daily Gazette* sells twice as many copies every day as any other popular newspaper, and about ten times as many as the kind of newspapers you like. Same with the *Sunday Sun*. That's the answer. And we're showing 'em what they want. We're running a big campaign to get them these things, to give 'em a good time. And there won't be any trouble. Except with the usual handful. And we can prove they're simply standing in the way of the boys getting steady jobs and have a bit of fun they've earned. Now don't look so depressed, young man."

" Sorry ! Didn't know I was doing." Alan drank some brandy.

" Your mother told me you used to do some writing before you joined up. Highbrow stuff, eh? What are you going to do now? "

Alan said he didn't know. " I was messing about in an estate office but don't intend to go back."

" Quite right. Nothing there. Now I'll tell you what

I'll do. Listen to this, Don. I'll put you on the staff of the *Gazette*—special correspondent—signed stories—to go round talking to these boys who've come back with you —finding out what they do want. You put before 'em what we're trying to do for 'em—and if that's what they want, then they say so."

" And if it isn't? " Alan enquired.

Darrald grinned. " Think you've caught me, eh? You put before 'em what we're trying to do for 'em—and if it isn't what they want and they say so definitely, we'll print it. Now then ! That's surprised you, hasn't it? Well, that's the offer. And Don'll talk money to you. It's his job." He turned in his chair quite sharply, completely dismissing Alan. " Tom," he called to Sir Thomas Stanford-Rivers, " come here. I heard a funny little story in the House this morning."

Don Markinch took Alan away from the table, well out of hearing. " That's the Boss," he began, with a kind of gloomy pride. " He mightn't do a thing like this again for six months. Must be feeling good tonight. Down here in the country, relaxed. Wish I could feel relaxed. Well, let's cut it short. I must 'phone the office in a minute. We'll pay you thirty-five pounds a week and give you a reasonable expense sheet. You'll have to keep moving around but you can work that out with Farley at the office. Twelve weeks guaranteed. If we keep you on after that—and I can think of something else you might do once this story's cold—then you don't get less money and might easily get more. You report at the office about the middle of next week. What d'you say? "

Alan didn't know what to say. He felt rather tight. This machine-gun style of Markinch rattled him badly. He was still feeling the effects of Lord Darrald's immense impressiveness. He was elated by the thought that he could suddenly start earning so much money. Yet behind this elation was a sad darkness of the spirit, a threat of sickness and misery, like a rain-heavy night surrounding some fireworks and only waiting to extinguish them. And there simply wasn't time to find out exactly what all this meant, for here in this corner was Markinch blinking and twitching at him impatiently. " What d'you say, eh? "

" Well, thanks very much," Alan stammered, " but I haven't had time to think it over yet. Could I let you know? "

Markinch looked disgusted. " We like to work fast. Look, I'll be here till after lunch tomorrow. Suppose you give me a ring."

As soon as Alan reached the drawing-room, his mother gave him a quick little signal. " Did he say anything to you? " she whispered.

He tried not to show his irritation. " Yes, tell you afterwards."

She searched his face for news, decided that all was well, then beamed round the room like a little lighthouse. " We mustn't stay very much longer. Did you men leave Lord Darrald behind? "

" He and that chap Markinch, who is one of his editors, are probably ringing up Teheran and San Francisco." He looked across and saw Betty, who was listening to some heavy stuff from Gerald. She looked like Nimue or Morgan le Fay sitting beneath the never-fading apple-blossom of Avalon, and then spoilt it by winking at him.

" Did you enjoy your dinner, darling? " his mother asked. " Are you glad you came? "

Was he? He dismissed the second question for further consideration. " Oh, yes, very sumptuous."

" I think Ann's getting restless. As soon as Lord Darrald comes in—and really I think he might do his telephoning at some other time—we'd better go."

Twenty minutes later they were drifting down the great stone steps that led to the front terrace where the cars were parked. There was a moon somewhere and a glimmer of stars over the hills, but immediately above there was cloud, and on the terrace the night was darkish, cool, but already rich with Spring. Round them was a garden manured by at least twenty first-class directorships. No wonder the old magic and devilment were in the air. Gerald and Colonel Southam had gone to fuss with their cars. Lady Strete and Ann were already deep in a discussion of the evening.

" Hoy! " cried Betty softly, and led him round a convenient corner. " You remember when I winked at you. What were you thinking about me just then? "

He put his arms round her, held her tight, a delicious armful, and then kissed her enthusiastically. " Isn't time to tell you now."

" Well, listen," she said quickly, " come over to lunch tomorrow and tell me about everything. Just us. Daddy's away for the day. I'm supposed to be going away. And I'll go too and you won't see me for ages, if you don't come to lunch tomorrow."

" I'll be there," said Alan, in a fine state of excitement. They slipped back and joined the others. The cars were ready for them.

" Quite an evening—eh, old boy? " said Gerald as he steered down the drive behind the Southams.

Alan looked at the dancing little red eye of the Southam car. " Quite an evening," he agreed. He huddled down in his seat and tried to think. But thinking was rather difficult.

6

HERBERT looked into the kitchen. "I'm catching the bus into Lambury," he told his mother. "Is there anything you want?"

"There might be one or two things," she said. "But why are you going into Lambury?"

"Dad asked me to. One or two little jobs there I can do for him."

"Oh I see." She could not hide the relief she felt. "It wasn't your idea, Herbert."

He pretended not to understand what was happening in her mind. "No, it was Dad's idea. Why?"

She smiled. "I thought you might be going there to see some young woman."

He had not admitted this even to himself and so he was not likely to admit it to her. But he realised again that there was such a thing as feminine intuition. "Mother, you keep forgetting I've been away for years. Why, I don't know anybody in Lambury these days. As for young women—well, I ask you!"

"No good asking me," she replied calmly. "But Edna told me last night that she thought there was somebody."

Hello, Edna now! A pincers movement of feminine intuition. "She doesn't know what she's talking about," he said with some irritation.

"Well, I know what I'm talking about," Mrs. Kenford observed, giving him a shrewd look. "And I'll tell you this, Herbert. Though I made excuses for you last night —I mean, to your Dad and the others—I didn't think you behaved very nicely, suddenly going out and leaving us like that."

"I explained——"

"Yes, I know. And I'd explained for you before that.

But that doesn't alter the fact, Herbert." And she gave him another deeply enquiring look.

Could he try to tell her now what he had felt? No, this wasn't the right moment. Besides, there was the bus. "Look, Mother, I'll have to push off if I'm going to catch that bus. Now is there anything you want?"

"No, there isn't really." She smiled at him now, as if her whole mood had changed. "Off you go, and don't bother coming back to supper if you don't want to. Go to the pictures. I should. There's a nice picture theatre in Lambury now. And I believe there's a late bus on Fridays too. You enjoy yourself, Herbert."

He felt at once that large, irrational and inexplicable sense of relief and release which a man experiences when the probe of feminine intuition is suddenly withdrawn. "Righto, Mother!" he cried, and hurried off.

In the little group waiting for the bus at the cross-roads was a chap called Pellit who liked to hear himself talk. "Hello, Herbert! Didn't know you were back."

"Well, I am," said Herbert, who was not anxious to listen to Pellit all the way to Lambury.

"That's the idea," said Pellit. "Here, wasn't Eddie Mold in your lot?"

"Yes. Came back with me. What about him?"

"Throwing his weight about a bit, Eddie is," said Pellit.

Herbert was interested now. "Doesn't sound like Eddie. Saw a lot of him out there, and he's a decent quiet chap, Eddie. Unless of course anybody tries any funny business with him, and he loses his temper. I've seen him do that once or twice," Herbert continued slowly, "and the other people didn't enjoy it at all. Anything been happening?"

"I was in the *Sun* last night," said Pellit, explaining at once. "Here's the bus, though. Tell you when we're inside."

The bus was full and they had to stand. But that did not stop Pellit, who attached himself to Herbert as they pushed past the baskets and fat knees of the women and then swayed and joggled by his side. " I was in the *Sun* last night," he began again, in a kind of confidential roar, " and George Fisher—you remember George?—saw Eddie there, just as Eddie was going. Both of 'em must have had a few. And George says ' Look who's here— old Eddie ! ' and all that—quite friendly really, though fancying himself a bit as usual. And Eddie tells him to turn it up, and then gives him a shove that nearly knocks him silly and scatters half the bar. I thought for a minute there was going to be a free fight. But Eddie looks as if he's ready to murder somebody—you can imagine what he'd look like—and then when Joe Finch—he keeps the *Sun* now—tells Eddie to clear out, he tells Joe what he can go and do with himself and then does clear out. And I wasn't sorry neither."

The bus was rattling and swaying, and it was hard to talk properly. But Herbert contrived to bring himself nearer to Pellit and to ask without shouting: " Was Eddie's wife with him? "

Pellit grinned knowingly. " No, she wasn't. There's been a bit of talk about her, along with some others, and I fancy Eddie might have heard something. He'd been in a corner drinking by himself for an hour or two—and that's not a good sign, is it?—and he might easily have heard a few things, because one or two of 'em at the *Sun* are not too careful what they say."

" Say about what? "

Pellit winked and grinned but said nothing for a minute or two, for the bus was tearing along and it was quite impossible to talk quietly. Then the bus stopped and gave Pellit his chance. " You know we had the Yanks here for some time," he said softly. " And a lot of 'em were in the *Sun* every night, chucking their money about, and some of the women were in and out with 'em, taking anything they could get. And, if you ask me, that's what's wrong with poor Eddie."

" I see," said Herbert. The bus started again, rattling and joggling them harder than ever, and giving Herbert an excuse to drop the conversation. He did not want to say anything else or to hear any more. He began thinking about Eddie, remembering him waiting for the mail to be given out, laboriously scrawling his letters home. Then the grin on Eddie's face when he had first put on that new brown suit. And now Eddie was in the *Sun* looking ready to murder somebody. Herbert felt vaguely guilty, as if he ought to have looked after Eddie and hadn't, as if he'd sent Eddie far out on patrol without ammo or rations. Pellit was trying to talk to him again but he pretended not to be able to hear. He had to go on thinking and anyhow didn't want any more from Pellit.

But when the bus finally rolled into the market square at Lambury, Pellit caught him before he could get away. " Thought you'd like to know about poor Eddie," he said, with a hint of apology.

Herbert no longer tried to escape. " Yes. Glad you told me."

" Fact is," said Pellit confidentially, " and I've said it more than once—chaps like Eddie aren't going to find it so easy to settle down."

" Settle down to what? "

" Well—get into civvies again—and just settle down."

" It wouldn't be a bad idea," said Herbert sharply, looking him in the eye, " if instead of chaps like Eddie having to settle down, some of you people had to settle up."

" What d'you mean? " Pellit stared back at him.

" I don't know quite," replied Herbert frankly. " But this *poor Eddie* line doesn't appeal to me. Not from you. I've seen Eddie give up his place in the boat, from a bridgehead we couldn't hold and were being shelled and mortared to hell out of. I've seen Eddie—oh well, it doesn't matter." He ended impatiently.

" Now look, don't start blaming me," said Pellit. " I've done nothing to him."

" I know. Only you took the wrong line, as far as I'm concerned. You see, I know Eddie Mold now, and I don't know your lot at the *Sun*. Or put it this way—I'm one of the strangers too. So long ! "

The sight of the *Crown* across the square suddenly jerked him out of his irritation. The fact that it was solidly there gave him an intense feeling of satisfaction. As obstinate with himself as he often was with other people, he refused to let this feeling go without being examined. It was because of that girl, Doris Morgan. He must be barmy. Why start more arguments?

Nevertheless, after paying a call or two for his father and having some food at the Co-operative Cafe, he made his way back to the square and, with the deliberation of a man who is doing something that he wants to do much more than he will allow, entered the Saloon Bar of the *Crown*. There were more people than there had been the other afternoon, when he had gone in with Alan Strete and Eddie ; but there was no Doris Morgan. He told himself he was a fool for imagining that she would be there, and then went on to call himself a bigger fool for even wanting her to be there and being there himself. But for all that, he lingered over his glass of bitter for a gloomy long time. The people who were there seemed to him uninteresting and their conversation idiotic.

Fortunately he had some further business to do for his father, and this kept him until it was time for a cup of tea. The picture theatre did not begin its programme until half-past five, but it had a cafe that was open earlier, and there he had some tea and felt rather foolish and uncomfortable among a crowd of women and girls. He had seen plenty of film shows behind the lines but it seemed to him an age since he had last been inside a picture theatre in England. No doubt he was not in the right mood, but now that he was in a picture theatre in England he discovered that it was not really in England but in America. Herbert had no prejudice against America and the Americans. Whenever he had been alongside the American Army, he had enjoyed and admired its peculiar characteristics ; its odd mixture of the slapdash and free-and-easy with superb engineer's efficiency in battle ; its taut hard concentration on the job and its raging but baffled desire, when off the job, to have a roaring good time. No, the Yanks were all right. But Herbert could not see why, when at last Lambury had its picture theatre, that picture theatre should be really in the United States.

Some of the news reel was British, but the brisk and facetious commentator sounded as if he was sorry it was. The rest was all American. There was a serious short documentary film, which pointed out to the audience in Lambury how successful they had been in defending the American way of life, whose other name was Democracy. There was a short comic piece, all about a harassed dentist, his nagging wife, his immense mother-in-law, his insufferable brother-in-law ; which offered a tasty little slab of the American way of life. Then came the large serious slab, the feature film. It was a long but uncomplicated story about some marines, who were engaged in some rather rum but noisy operations, and their girl friends, who were quiet and almost angelic nurses by day and apparently loud jitterbug queens at night. If anybody ever went home, he or she climbed great staircases, walked down vast corridors, and then entered cosy little rooms about a hundred-and-fifty feet long. When the marines were not sweating in a dim jungle or trying to dodge tropical downpours that seemed to follow them about, they were trying to forget it all, in colossal night-clubs where the floor-shows appeared to cover the area of a football ground. Sometimes the girls took temperatures and smoothed pillows in a sad refined manner, but it was impossible to imagine them doing anything with blood-soaked dressings or bed pans, which is probably why they seemed to be so gay and tireless at night, shaking their faultless curls in front of famous swing bands. It was all quite unlike any kind of war and wartime that Herbert could possibly believe in, and if it was just expensive non-sense, and not even a specimen of the American way of life, then there seemed to him no reason why it should have been imported all the way from Hollywood to Lambury. Whether the rest of the people there felt as he did, he could not discover, for they neither clapped nor booed, nor showed any sign of approval or disapproval, but just sat there dimly staring and listening. Instead of being out to enjoy themselves, they might have been sitting in a doctor's waiting-room. But perhaps they were not trying to enjoy themselves but were merely passing the time—as he was. The English way of life. But why import all that muck?

It was just after eight when he reached the *Crown* again. Nothing quiet about it this time. Friday night and plenty of money about. Now the Saloon Bar looked like a hot packed cave. Too much smoke, too much noise, too many people. He had to push his way through to the bar, and had to wait some time before he could be served. Then he saw her, Doris Morgan. She was wearing the same yellow scarf. She was with a whole gang, youngish chaps and girls and a few middle-aged persons too. They all obviously knew each other very well. Probably all from the aircraft factory. And they were working so hard at being jolly that they were almost sure to be celebrating some occasion. Doris Morgan was doing her share, shouting at this one and laughing with that one ; and Herbert guessed that she had had her share of the drinks too. While he was still staring across at her, he began to wonder why he had bothered about her.

" You don't want all the bar, do you mister? " said a man at his elbow.

" Yes," said Herbert sourly, giving him a hard look.

" Now look," said the man, changing his tone, " I'm only——"

" All right," said Herbert, " help yourself." He moved aside. " Only—next time—don't talk like that."

He stared across at the girl again, and this time she saw him. He saw her frown, as if trying to remember where she had seen him before, and then her face cleared, as if she suddenly remembered ; and she smiled at him. He gave her a nod, took a sip of his beer and looked away. Nothing to get excited about.

Two minutes later she was by his side, almost jammed against him. Her eyes were not as dark as they seemed to be at a distance. They were a warm glinting brown. " By yourself this time? " she was asking.

" Yes," he replied. Then added fatuously : " Just looked in for a drink."

" Well, I didn't think you'd come in for a wash and brush up. Like to join the party? "

" No, thanks. Too many of you."

" Oh well—if that's how you feel." She turned, trying to attract the attention of the barmaid.

He waited a moment. " I came in here earlier today."

" Oh, did you? " She was not interested.

But she had to be interested, and it was now or never.

" I came in looking for you. That's why I came back tonight."

" Go on! " But now she really looked at him. " I believe you did too."

" I've just told you, haven't I? " he said with some irritation.

" Yes, but I don't believe all I'm told. But if you did then why did you? "

" Because I've been thinking about you, and about what you said the other afternoon—d'you remember ? " He was eager, friendly now.

But somehow it didn't work. " No, I don't remember," she said sulkily, not responding at all.

" All right, it doesn't matter," he said angrily, looking away. " Go back and get pickled. You've still plenty of time."

" Haven't you a temper? " she cried. " You were just the same the other day. Took me up and glared at me."

" I thought you said you didn't remember."

" I remember what you were like. Wouldn't have asked you to join us, if I hadn't remembered you, would I? Your name's Herbert Kenford and you come from a farm at Crowfield. See? "

" And your name's Doris Morgan, and you work at the aircraft factory, which is just closing down. And I told you that you were in a bad temper, and you said When you do start thinking, just get it right.' See? "

She smiled now, and it was a warm friendly smile. ' And you said, ' Get what right? ' and I said, ' Everything. You'll see.' Isn't that right? "

" Yes, it is," he assured her earnestly. "And I'm glad you remember."

" Well, what do we do now? You won't join our little

lot——"

" I'm sorry, but I just don't feel like it tonight."

" Well, you might be surprised to hear that I don't much myself. But we can't do much talking like this y'know. And it'll be worse soon."

" I know it will," he said gloomily. " And I've had enough of this place already. I hate crowded pubs.' He left the next move to her.

She thought for a moment. " Look, if you'll wait about ten minutes for me, we'll go out and talk. I can't come out at once because this is my round and I must attend to it. Wait outside, then I can make some excuse and won't have to take any nasty cracks about going off with a strange young man. Right? " She began to clamour for the attention of the barmaid.

It seemed a long ten minutes out there in the darkening street, so long that he began to think she had been fooling him. When at last the door did swing back and he saw her, trim and smiling in the light, there came to him, like a blue bubble, a moment of pure happiness. Eagerly and gratefully he welcomed her.

" I know it's been more than ten minutes," she confessed, as they moved off, " but I was lucky to get away at all. Felt a bit mean about it too. I may not see some of those people again and we've all been working together. Where are we going? "

" I don't mind. Anywhere it's quiet."

" All right. But look, when I said talking, I meant talking—and nothing else. I've had enough mauling about and I'm off it. So don't say I didn't warn you."

Coming so soon after the magical moment in the doorway, this speech of hers was all wrong and made him angry. " And when I said talking, I meant talking too. I don't want to maul you about—as you call it—and I'm sorry to hear so many other chaps have had a go at it."

"I didn't say they had. I only said I'd had enough of it to last me some time. And don't keep losing your temper. I never knew such a chap! What happens down there?"

"Canal," said Herbert sulkily. "We can walk along it—unless you think I'll throw you in."

"I'll have to risk that," she said gaily, as if they were old friends now. As they turned down the narrow side-street, where the night was gathering, she took his arm in the most natural and easy fashion. "Before we forget —are you catching that last bus? Well, so am I. I get off just before the cross-roads."

He was glad to hear this, and said so. It meant that he could see her to her digs, wherever they were, and then easily walk home. They would have to be careful about catching the bus, that was all. But he didn't have to cram all he had to say into the next hour. He explained this too.

"Righto," she said comfortably. "Only I can't be kept out half the night, y'know, silly as I look. And when we're talking, just remember that you've had one glass of beer—that was it, wasn't it?—whereas I've had about six gin-and-limes."

"And that's about four too many," he said earnestly.

"Pack it up," she warned him.

He said nothing, and after a moment or two the fingers resting on his arm gave it a little squeeze. He produced a little chuckle, rather to his own surprise. They were now walking by the canal. Everything was quiet and still, and there was a mixed smell of paint, rotten old timbers, and canal water.

"You're a serious chap, aren't you?"

"Yes I am," he replied at once. She might as well know.

"I saw you were, right at the first," she said. "Quite

101

different from the other one—the good-looking one with the smile."

"Quite different. He's a grand chap," Herbert added. "Alan Strete. All the girls go for him, of course."

"I wouldn't," she said promptly. "As for you—I feel about you that I'd either like you a lot or hate the sight of you. I don't know which yet. Look, let's sit down here and have a smoke."

They sat on some old timber and smoked. Then he began to talk to her, hesitatingly at first but gathering confidence as he went along. He told her about the supper at home the night before.

"What's she like, this Edna?" she asked, interrupting him.

"Oh, she's all right, but not my style."

"What *is* your style?"

"Oh, I don't know, but she isn't," he replied with some impatience. "But she's not important. She's not the point."

"No, I suppose not," said Doris slowly, as if reluctant to leave the subject. "Well—go on."

"You see," he continued, "when I saw they'd made all these plans for me—buying the other farm for my brother Arthur, keeping Four Elm for me to take over gradually—I felt ashamed of myself."

"You needn't have been," she said quickly. "They hadn't asked you what you wanted. They were only making sure they'd got the family all properly planted."

"Then afterwards, when they began to spread themselves a bit, specially my father, I suddenly felt different. They just didn't seem to care about what happened to anybody else so long as we were all right."

"Are you telling me?" she cried.

"It was all wrong. It wasn't what I expected at all. Of course the army's different, with discipline and tasks and targets and all that, but even so, if we'd gone on this 'Damn you, I'm all right' tack, we'd never have done the job and the whole spirit would have been different. And we were told all the time that people here at home weren't the same as they used to be——"

" Some of 'em aren't," she told him.

" Well, naturally I expected to notice this difference as soon as I got home. Several things that happened before I actually got home made me feel a bit uneasy. But I didn't take much notice of them. But then—when they all sat there, round our old table, all so pleased that they'd got a good fat share and all so determined to stick to it whatever happened to everybody else—I suddenly felt terribly about it. I say," he added awkwardly, " I feel it's a bit rotten talking like this. They're my own folks—and they're very fond of me—and they're good people really—and I don't want you to get the wrong idea." His voice trailed off rather helplessly.

" I'm not going back on what I said right at the first —I mean, about talking and not anything else. Even if I am a wee bit tight. So don't take any notice. But I must do this." And she leaned over and kissed him gently. " That's because I like you. No, there won't be any more, not tonight. Talk—talk."

" I don't know how that other chap you saw, Alan Strete, is going on," he continued, rather breathless after this surprising interlude. " I'm going to ask him. But I heard something this morning about the third chap who came back with me—d'you remember him?—big burly chap." And he told her what he had heard about Eddie Mold.

" I could have told you plenty about that sort of carry on," she said quietly. " Enough to fill ten dirty books. I've been about where it's been happening. Oh—it's a mess all right, and I'm not pretending it isn't. Though it's not really as bad as it looks—some women just can't stand the dreariness and loneliness after a year or two—they've got to have something happening. Your chap—and all of 'em—ought to try to forgive and forget and start all over again. We're all a bit weak and daft and we've had so much to take. But listen——" and she jumped up and screwed a fierce little hand into his coat—" it isn't that that worries me—that could be all over and done with soon—it's what you were talking about before—all that damned stupid greedy selfishness that's starting all over again. I tell you, the minute the real danger passed, and people felt safe again, out it came. Nothing's happened to them inside. They haven't changed. They haven't learnt anything—except how to make bigger and bigger bombs and hate like hell. And where's that going to take us? What's next. Oh—damn and blast——! "

" Are you crying? " asked Herbert, astonished.

" Yes, you fathead. Hold me a minute—and shut up. Yes, I know I said you couldn't—but this is different—and you're different too."

So there they were, by the dim canal, the night settling round them, while she sniffed a little and his heart thumped away. All of it was a complete surprise to Herbert, who had forgotten—if he had ever known before—how odd and unexpected girls could be. He could not have said whether he was enjoying himself or not. This experience had to be judged somewhere on the other side of mere enjoyment.

" What time is it? " she asked, withdrawing herself. " We ought to be making for that bus."

When they started to walk back she was silent and did not take his arm again. The little gap between them seemed to be immense. He did not like this, and after a minute or two he took her hand and tucked it inside his arm. Then they were all right again.

104

"I wish you'd tell me something about yourself," he said, after some hesitation. "I know your name's Doris Morgan and that you've been working at the aircraft factory and that you used to work in a shop and lived in Croydon. And I remember what you said about your brothers," he added quietly.

"Fancy you remembering all that!" she said, as if grateful to him.

"Well, of course I do. But I'd like to know a lot more. I've been talking about myself but you haven't told me anything really about your life—have you?"

"There isn't a lot," she said vaguely. And then, to his surprise and rather to his annoyance, she took a wild jump back to Edna. "I suppose this Edna was brought up on a farm, eh?"

"Yes, partly anyhow. But never mind about her. She doesn't come into it."

Another wild jump now. "Do you like farming, Herbert?"

"I don't mind the work, though it's pretty hard. But it's what I've been used to." There he stopped.

"Go on. Tell me a bit more about it."

"Well, I haven't—sort of—worked it out in my mind yet," he said slowly, carefully. "The job's all right. I think I'd rather do that than anything else. It's good work, y'know, farming. Something satisfying about it. You'd understand that if you'd lived on a farm."

"I'll bet I wouldn't," she said mournfully. "I'll bet it would give me the creeps."

This made him feel depressed too. They were talking as if they belonged to two different nations. He saw her for an instant against an alien background of huge factories, glittering shops, streets and crowds, flashy pubs, Croydon, London.

"I'll bet this Edna——" she began.

5

"Oh—blow Edna! I keep telling you she doesn't come into it. Forget her."

She squeezed his arm. "Old Narky, aren't you? All right, we'll forget her. Go on about farming. What's wrong with it?"

"I never said there was anything wrong with it."

"No, you didn't say it, but you sounded as if you thought there was. Tell it by your voice. See?"

"Well, it's something I never felt before I joined up," he said, returning to his slow careful manner. "But coming back this time, I've felt it all right. It seems to cut you off too much. After a time, if you don't look out, you don't seem to care what's happening to other people. You aren't part of anything. You're out for yourself—and just your family. Mind you, it's easy to feel like that— because you have to work hard and it takes nearly all your time—and you don't meet many people who are doing different jobs, the way you do in towns. But it's not right somehow. It shouldn't be like that. We've had enough of that. Like you said, if we're going back to all that, I don't know where we'll be."

The bus was there, and they ran to make sure of catching it. Herbert wondered if some of her gang from the pub would be in the bus. If they were, how would she behave? He felt that this was important, a kind of test. No sooner were they inside than he noticed about half-a-dozen of the gang, crowded together, cheerful and noisy, sitting at the back. They shouted and waved at Doris, but she only gave them a little smile and a nod, then turned to the nearest empty seat, where there was room for him too. And he experienced again that immense sense of relief, melting into pure happiness, which had come to him when she appeared in the doorway of the *Crown*.

They said very little in the bus as it rattled and swayed

and roared through the night. She looked tired now, almost exhausted, the light from above hollowing out her face and emptying it of all vitality. She became small, fragile, precious. Now and then, when their glances met, she smiled at him, perhaps to keep something companionable in their silence, but the smile seemed to him far-away, ghostly, rather frightening. He felt a bit tired too, but he was anxious not to let go of the evening, not to allow her to slip away, for he felt that she might disappear for ever, be lost to him for ever and ever in some distant glitter of factories and shops and streets and bars. . . .

" I get out here," she said.

" I'm coming with you."

" Let's hurry then or some of that crowd will grab me."

They hurried down the dark road for a minute or two. Then they turned down a lane, where, Herbert remembered, some cottages had been put up just before the war. Now they walked slowly, close together in the wide sweet-smelling night. It was best of all here.

She was quite different from the fierce challenging creature he had gone into Lambury to find. It was surprising how quickly she could change. But now he felt that this was not because she herself was odd but because women were different from men, and that at last, through her, he was beginning to appreciate this huge significant fact.

" Look, Herbert," she said quietly, " I talk a lot—and they say I throw my weight about and lay down the law —but I don't suppose I'm much good really. You ask that sour-faced old barmaid at the *Crown*—she'll tell you."

" I wouldn't ask her about anything," said Herbert, " specially about you. Leave her out of it."

" No, but I've spent a lot of time—and money, 'cos I pay my share—in there, and one or two other places, just wasting my evenings. And I say everything's rotten and we ought to get together to make it better—and I mean it too—but what have I done about it, beyond talking a lot and getting up once or twice at the factory meetings? I don't know much, but I don't really try to learn. I did all right at the factory, but that was easy."

"Even if it was," said Herbert, defending her against herself, "it can't have been easy being away from home all this time, and knowing everything back home had been blitzed, and—and your brothers and all that. Just dumped down here to work, wondering about everything —no, Doris, that can't have been easy."

"You're sweet, Herbert, you really are. I didn't think you'd be. I knew you'd be —sort of—steady and reliable —but not like this. Look!" And she stopped, grasped his coat with both hands, and kissed him as she had done by the canal. "No, let me talk a bit. While I have a chance. You see, I'm twenty-six. How old are you?"

"Twenty-seven," replied Herbert promptly. Then he laughed. "You sounded as if you were fifty."

"That's what I feel like sometimes. As if it's nearly all gone by, while I've been working in that Assembly Shop or gassing and having drinks at places like the *Crown*. It seems years and years since I lived at home and worked in the shop. I didn't know anything at all then."

"You say you don't know much now," he told her.

"No, that's different, silly. I don't know much now about the things people ought to know about—politics and economics and all that."

"Well, neither do I, though they told us a bit in the army. But we can learn."

"I ought to have learnt now," she said, rather fiercely. "That's what I'm telling you. But before I meant I didn't know anything about life in general. What people

108

really think and feel, what they're up to, how chaps behave—and all that."

"I don't like this part about chaps," he said solemnly. "No, I'm not being funny——"

"I know you're not, Herbert, I just had to laugh—you sounded so miserable. Look, that's my billet—second house. Mrs. Thompson. She hated me at first, but now we get on all right. Most people aren't so bad when you really get to know them, are they? I mean, even if they do things and say things you don't like, you begin to understand why. Mrs. Thompson thinks that if she doesn't put that silly old Tory back into Parliament, then everything will be divided up and probably Mrs. Flanagan next-door will get one of her two pink vases. You can't argue with her. But never mind about Mrs. Thompson. Let's stop here a minute, then I must go in."

So there they stayed, each of them staring at the strange dim oval of the other's face, staring and wondering, waiting for some miracle of understanding and tenderness.

"Well?" And it came from her almost like a sigh. "Well?" And even in this one short word the strain in his voice was apparent.

That is all they said for a few moments but the air between them was thick with unspoken questions. What am I? What are you? What do you think of me? What shall we do?

But now her mood changed again and she was unexpectedly fierce and challenging. "Look, Herbert, whatever you do, don't go back on what you're beginning to feel now. Don't let 'em make you comfortable. Don't let 'em stop you thinking. Don't let 'em persuade you we can go in the same old way, not caring what happens to other people. We're all tied up together, Herbert. We can't help it—that's our life—and if we aren't all together, working and thinking for each other, then it's all hate and misery and bloody murder—honest to God it is."

" I think you're right, Doris. I haven't worked it out yet—don't seem to have had time—but that's the way I'm beginning to feel. But—y'know—just coming home——"

" I know, I know," she cried in a fierce whisper. " You've been away fighting. You want to be quiet for a bit and take it easy. Of course you do—it's only natural. But while you're taking it easy, Herbert, they'll take the heart out of you. Don't bother about me—unless you want to—but for God's sake—stand up straight, keep yourself really alive, and just do a bit more fighting—for all of us. We may not seem worth it—but we are really —just because our life is your life too, and if you begin to cut yourself off you begin to die. That's the way it is, Herbert. Look, I must go in."

He squeezed her shoulders gently. " I don't want to search the pubs for you——"

" And I don't want you to. You know where I live now—at Mrs. Thompson's here—Number Five. Though I shan't be here very much longer."

" Then can I see you tomorrow—it's Saturday? "

" No," she told him quietly, very solemn now. " It isn't that I'm doing anything else or don't want to see you. I do. But it's too soon. Do you see what I mean, Herbert? I want to think about you a bit. I want you to think about me. And not rush it."

" Yes, but you say you won't be here much longer. Sunday then—Sunday afternoon—please."

She hesitated a moment. " All right then. About half-past two—here. Good-night, Herbert."

" Good-night, Doris."

He heard her close the door before he moved. It was only about a couple of miles to Four Elm and he hardly noticed them, walking in a dream. But in the dream there rose the sad bewilderment that a man feels when he moves from one world into another, from a little patch of night that should have been home but was not home yet, only a dim face and whispering under the stars, to the fireside and the bed that were home once but could never be home again. A young man in a grey suit, back from the wars, yet already lost. . . .

7

ABOUT ten o'clock on Friday night Eddie Mold came lumbering up the road towards his cottage. He wasn't drunk and he wasn't sober, he was all muddled. He had been away from home all day, out of Crowfield too, wandering about, bewildered and resentful. He had finished up by having several pints in a mournful dirty little beer-house just off the Bancester road, where he had had a long confused argument with a couple of farm hands, and when they had turned nasty he had turned nastier still, asking the pair of them to come outside. The landlady—an unpleasant fat woman who hadn't liked the look of Eddie from the first—had told him to take himself off and go back to where he belonged ; and everybody else there had been on her side. Nobody was on Eddie's side.

There was nothing at home to cheer him up. Somehow it looked worse than it had done when he had left it that morning, more neglected and forlorn, as if something hostile, some influence of the mysterious new enemy that seemed to menace him now from all sides, had been at work all day on the place, making it look less and less like a real home. He looked round in disgust : it didn't

111

seem to belong to him any more. He was tired after wandering about nearly all day, but he didn't feel like sleep. And he wanted to talk to somebody, somebody decent who would be friendly. The only person he could think of was poor Fred Roseberry's widow, only a few doors away. He had noticed a light in her window as he passed, and though it was getting late, he thought he might chance it.

When he saw her standing there in the lighted doorway, quiet and neat, puzzled and a bit afraid, he wondered vaguely if he had done wrong to go there.

" Oh, it's you, Mr. Mold," she said, relieved when she recognised him. She hesitated a moment. " Well, you'd better come in."

He followed her inside, feeling large and clumsy and not too clean. He hadn't shaved for the last two days and it occurred to him now that his new brown suit must be looking as if he'd slept in it in a ditch. She'd been listening to the wireless and doing some sewing. While she switched off the wireless, he took a quick look round the room, which was both tidy and cosy, very different from the forlorn cold place he had just left.

" You sit down there, Mr. Mold," she said, and sat down herself and took up her sewing again. They both settled down. " I suppose you've come to ask about your wife."

" Yes, that's right," he mumbled, glancing shyly across at her pale serious face.

" Well, she stayed here," replied Mrs. Roseberry gravely, looking rather hard at him, " and then this morning she went back to her mother's. She was terribly upset, you know."

It wasn't easy to talk properly in here, and anyhow he was tired, a bit stupid after all that beer, all muddled too. " Well, so was I," he muttered. " So would you 'ave been. Way she'd gone on."

Mrs. Roseberry put down her sewing. "I'm not saying she did right, Mr. Mold. I know she didn't. I told her so. The way a lot of them went on—I was ashamed and disgusted. But it was a bit different for her—it was really, Mr. Mold." She regarded him solemnly. She had fine dark eyes, some colour in her cheeks too, and seemed far better-looking than usual.

"Why was it?" He sounded surly.

She hesitated. "Because of her losing her baby. She told me that made all the difference to her, and I'm sure it would. I know it's the children that have kept me going. Without them to look after, I don't know what I'd have done. And when a woman loses her baby—and her husband's a long way off, and the war goes on and on—well, she can easily get desperate. A woman needs somebody—and if she hasn't anybody—and she's miserable and has nothing to look forward to—then she might do nearly anything for a bit of excitement. There really is some excuse for her, Mr. Mold."

He took some time to consider this ; his mind was working very slowly. "Might 'ave been some excuse for a break-out just once," he said carefully. "But not for going on and on with it."

"How do you know she did go on and on with it?"

"By them bottles," he replied. "Besides the talk I 'eard."

"I wouldn't take too much notice of the talk you hear," she warned him. "Some of them'll say anything."

"What's the matter with 'em round 'ere?" he demanded angrily. "They've made it a thousand times worse—with their slurs an' nasty sly looks. What 'ave I done to 'em? Are they all diff'rent or is it me?"

She looked at him sympathetically but did not reply.

"I tell yer this, Mrs. Roseberry," he said, much quieter

now. " If she'd been waitin' for me when I come back
—an' she'd said to me what she seems to 'ave said to you
—or at any rate what you've just told me—about 'er bein'
upset about the kid an' all that—an' then said ' I did
wrong, Eddie, an' I'm sorry' or something like that—
then it'ud 'ave been diff'rent as far as I'm concerned.
But she wasn't even 'ere. She opened my tellygram an'
then left it fastened again, to pretend she 'adn't seen it.
Then she comes back—to start pretendin' nothing's
'appened——"

" I know, I know," cried Mrs. Roseberry. " She managed it all wrong. She knows that now."

"An' I'll bet she does." He could sit still no longer.
He stood, swaying a little, staring down at the floor while
he tried to find words that would tell her what he felt.
As his resentment began boiling up, he had to begin
moving, and he took several turns up towards the door
and back before he faced her again.

" I wish yer could 'ave 'eard us chaps talkin' out there
about what it'ud be like when we got back. 'Ours an'
'ours of it. Whatever we got started on, it nearly always
come back to that. *You wait, boys!* Well I come back,
never feelin' better in my life, in civvies again, friends
with everybody. An' it's all gone wrong, every dam' bit
of it—an' honestly, now an' again, when it all comes over
me, Mrs. Roseberry, I feel like bloody murder."

" No, no." She was standing now, and sounded dis-
tressed.

" Excuse the language, Mrs. Roseberry," he said apologetically. " Didn't mean it. Beg pardon!"

" It isn't that, Mr. Mold," she cried earnestly, regard-
ing him with pity. " I understand what you feel—but it
isn't as bad as you think, none of it—really it isn't."

Perhaps it was the pity in her eyes that did it. Or just
the mere sight of her standing there, a fine-looking

friendly woman. He went towards her, not knowing exactly what he would do, but with his hands reaching out in front of him. He saw her start back, caught a flicker of fear—and it might be disgust too—in her eyes, and he stopped dead.

"I want to talk to you sometime about Fred," she stammered. "But it's too late tonight. I think you'd better go now, hadn't you, Mr. Mold?"

"Yes, I'd better go," he muttered, not even looking at her any more. "Good-night."

He lumbered back to his own cottage, feeling a ton-weight of misery. Everything he did was wrong. There seemed to be no place he could go where he'd be all right. Any evening in a lousy billet out of mortar range had been better than anything that had happened to him yet round here. God's truth, he'd felt better than he felt now even with his guts quivering in a slit trench. Be-wildered, brooding, he went to bed. Sleep, sleep—it couldn't come too soon. But it was some time before it did.

Saturday morning, and not a bit like it. Nothing to eat for breakfast because he'd forgotten to buy anything. He couldn't bring himself to go along to the village, so although he felt very hungry he did without food and merely had a good strong brew-up of tea and a smoke. After this he took a long surly look round and decided to clean the place up a bit. He was in the middle of this job, bad-tempered on it but fairly thorough, when unfor-tunately his first visitor arrived, giving a knock on the half-open front door and then walking in. It was the parson, Mr. Drawden, white-haired now but still rosy and smiling. He hadn't missed his breakfast.

"Well, well!" cried Mr. Drawden in his cheeriest manner. "We're hardly back before we're doing our share of the housework. But it's nothing to you fellows who've been in the army, eh? And how are you?"

"All right," Eddie muttered.

"Mrs. Mold out doing the shopping, I suppose—eh?"

"No, she isn't. She's gone to her mother's."

Mr. Drawden sat down, laid his hat across his plump thighs, placed a large white hand on each side of the hat, took the smile off his face, and stared solemnly at Eddie "I'm sorry to hear that. I'd gathered—in a rather round-about fashion—that you'd had some trouble here, and it's one reason why I called this morning. I'd hoped that it wasn't true—there's a good deal of foolish gossip in the village these days—but now, I imagine, it must be."

"That's right," Eddie told him, wooden-faced. "Been some trouble."

Mr. Drawden put the smile on again. "Now suppose we light our pipes and just talk it over quietly."

"You light yours if you want to," Eddie said drily, "but I 'aven't got one."

"Cigarette then? Have some somewhere."

"No, thanks all the same. Don't feel like smokin'." He didn't feel like talking either, his manner added.

Mr. Drawden did a big act with his pipe and pouch, almost as if giving a demonstration. "We have to think things over—yes, and talk things over—at these times. This war of course has been a long interruption in all our lives——"

"No, not all?"

"Why? I don't quite follow you there, Mold."

"A lot of blokes I used to know an' was with out there, the war 'asn't interrupted their lives. It's finished 'em."

"Well, I don't agree that it's finished them—and I'm sorry to learn that you think it has—but I see what you mean. Still, for most of us the war has been, as I said, a long interruption in our lives——"

"And another thing," said Eddie doggedly. "I

thought that after this war the idea was to make a sort of fresh start."

"Yes, yes—oh certainly," said Mr. Drawden heartily. "We all hope that that will be possible—to a certain extent. The Government has definite plans. But no doubt you've heard about them."

"Yes, I've 'eard about 'em."

"But now we're talking about more personal matters," Mr. Drawden continued rather hastily, as if he did not like Eddie's dubious tone. "You've had some trouble here, but I hope that it will be possible to put everything right very soon. A little patience," he suggested hopefully. "More understanding of each other's worries and difficulties. A spirit of forgiveness and Christian charity on both sides, eh?"

Eddie made no reply. Mr. Drawden filled in the awkward gap by doing some elaborate pipe-lighting.

"We see you young fellows come back to us," said Mr. Drawden, forcing a smile, "so many conquering heroes——"

"We're not conquerin' 'eroes," cried Eddie. "I'm no 'ero. Never wanted to be."

"Quite so. That's our British attitude——"

"Never mind that, Mr. Drawden. I can't see British attitudes is much diff'rent from other chap's attitudes—except Nazis, an' they're just plain barmy. But I'm no 'ero. I'm just an ordinary chap come back from a lot o' muck an' blood an' flamin' murder. I've seen places so flattened out yer wouldn't know if you was lookin' at the Town 'All or a pig stye. I've seen blokes burnt alive. It didn't ought to 'ave 'appened——"

"Certainly it oughtn't," said Mr. Drawden soothingly. "But then, you see, the Nazis——"

"I know about them. I've 'eard it all," cried Eddie. "An' I've seen 'em. They're barmy. But what beats me is why anybody ever thought they were anything else. Who let 'em loose? Who give 'em such a nice start? These blokes like 'Itler an' 'Immler, why wasn't they put in lunatic asylums or 'anged as bloody murderers years an' years since? Who fixed it so I spend years of my life chasin' them fellers?"

"That's really a political question," said Mr. Drawden. "We made mistakes, of course——"

"Well I don't 'ear any o' these big pots tellin' us they made any mistakes. Old What's-it 'ere—our M.P.—'e doesn't come to me an' say, 'Look, Eddie Mold, I made a lot o' mistakes an' I'm sorry.' Not likely! But that's all over an' done with, yer say, an' now we'll make a fresh start. But who's makin' this fresh start? Tell me just a few 'ere in Crowfield. What are they doin' an' 'ow are they doin' it? I can tell yer what some of 'em are doin' but there's no fresh start about that. Yer might think I'd just come back from doin' time the way some of 'em look an' talk. An' it's all just as wrong as the muck an' murder we've left. What we want—what I want——" He stopped for a moment, to grapple with his thought.

It was at that moment that Sergeant Parkinson, of the Banfordshire County Police, arrived. Parkinson had been a constable when Eddie joined the army, but now he was a sergeant. Eddie knew him of old, and had never liked him. There had always been something officious and hostile about Bert Parkinson even when he was only a constable. Now, after promotion, he was not likely to be any better. Moreover he had interrupted Eddie just when Eddie was trying to say something important.

"That's right," Eddie said to him with heavy sarcasm, "just walk in."

"Door was open," said Sergeant Parkinson. "Oh—

118

good morning, Mr. Drawden. Didn't know you were here."

"Course you didn't," cried Eddie indignantly, staring hard at the policeman's big leathery face. "You didn't give yourself time to know who was 'ere. Well, what d'yer want?"

The sergeant looked apologetically at Mr. Drawden, who showed no sign of moving. "Not important. It'll do some other time."

"Go on," said Eddie. "Let's 'ave it."

"If you think you'd be better without me," Mr. Drawden began.

"Matter of fact, it might help a bit, so far as I'm concerned," said Sergeant Parkinson, "if you stayed and listened, Mr. Drawden."

"Well—in that case——" said Mr. Drawden smiling.

Eddie glanced irritably from one to the other of these two visitors. They seemed to be getting on very cosily together, settling down nicely, you might say; but where did he come in?

Sergeant Parkinson cleared his throat, looked hard at Eddie for a moment or two, then began ponderously: "I've just had one or two complaints about you, Eddie Mold. One about the way you were carrying on in the *Sun*, the other night. Bad language and threatening violence. Well, I let that pass. But now I've had another complaint. Out at the *Bell* last night. Same thing too."

"Yes, an' I've got something to say." This came from a voice at the door. It was Mrs. Mogson.

"Pop off, you!" shouted Eddie, all the angrier because this interruption had startled him. "Go on, sharp!"

"You see," cried the old woman to both the State and the Church. "I can do some complainin' too. Shoutin' 'is 'ead off—all sorts of language—late at night, wakin'

119

me an' my daughter up. Shameful! We've 'ad one sort o' carryings-on 'ere, an' now it's another sort."

She gave a screech and stepped back as Eddie made a sudden rush at the door. All he meant to do was to shut it in her wicked old face, but she behaved as if she thought he was going to knock her down. Sergeant Parkinson hastily intervened, but Eddie managed to shut the old woman out.

"That's all I want to do," he explained. "Shut 'er out. I won't 'ave that mischief-makin' old devil screamin' on my doorstep."

"Well, you might be right as far as that's concerned," said the sergeant heavily. "But that's another one complaining, you see? You see, Mr. Drawden?"

"Yes, yes, yes," said Mr. Drawden hastily. "Great pity. Very great pity. What were you going to say, Sergeant?"

"I just want to say this to him," said Sergeant Parkinson, as if Eddie wasn't really there.

"Well, say it whatever it is," cried Eddie. "For God's sake, say it an' go."

"More language now. You'll be forgetting who's with us in a minute." The sergeant was shocked. "And what I want to say is this. You're not in the army now, Eddie Mold. You're a civilian and you'll behave yourself like a civilian. And if you don't, then you'll get into trouble—real trouble. Don't think you can come here and do as you like——"

"Do as I like?" Eddie was furious. "Do as I like? I 'aven't done anything yet I even wanted to do. Not a flamin' rotten thing."

Mr. Drawden held up his large white hand, to check both Eddie and Sergeant Parkinson, who was about to make a sharp reply. "Now, now—you really mustn't lose your temper like this. Sergeant Parkinson is telling you something for your good, just giving you a friendly warning——"

"Well, 'e can take 'is friendly warnings somewhere else," Eddie shouted. "I don't 'ave to 'ave police sergeants walkin' in on me. Nor parsons neither for that matter——"

"That's enough. That's quite enough," said Mr. Drawden, rising with enormous dignity. He turned to the sergeant. "There's been some domestic trouble here, Sergeant, and I'd hoped that we might have smoked a pipe or two together and talked as man to man——"

"Well, I don't want to smoke a pipe an' talk as man to man," Eddie roared out of his vast wilderness of anger and frustration.

"What you want to do and what you ought to do are two very different things," said Sergeant Parkinson sternly. "You won't listen to Mr. Drawden here. You won't listen to me——"

"That's right. And I won't listen to old Mrs. Mogson next door neither. So that makes three of yer I won't listen to. An' no doubt there's a hell of a lot more I won't listen to. So push off." He glared at them for a moment. Then the whole raw bleeding misery inside him seemed to explode. "What's the matter with you all? Are you all goin' barmy—or am I? 'Cos honest to God I don't know where I am. An' if I 'ave much more of this, I don't know what I'll do to somebody."

"You'll do nothing to anybody," said Sergeant Parkinson, opening the door for Mr. Drawden. "And I give you no more warnings, remember. After you, Mr. Drawden."

Mr. Drawden turned to give Eddie a last reproachful look. "Just try and reflect now. Remember your new responsibilities, Mold. And if at any time——"

"Good-mornin'," cried Eddie, and then turned his

back on them. He was angry with them, particularly with Parkinson ; but he was also angry with himself too. He knew he was not behaving properly, but it seemed now as if he couldn't behave properly, as if there was some huge mysterious conspiracy to put him in the wrong, even with himself.

After brooding over all this for some time he returned to the task of cleaning and tidying the cottage. It was something to do. And if he could not clear up the dreary muddle in his mind, at least he could clear up the dreary muddle in the kitchen. And then, taking everything out of the big cupboard, he made a discovery. At the back, behind two canisters, he found a half-bottle of whisky, the flat flask type, and it was nearly full. He had a preliminary sniff at it to make sure it really was whisky. Then he had a sip, to make doubly sure. It was whisky all right, and good whisky too. Well, he could drink whisky ; and he did. He drank it all in great fiery gulps.

People stared at him when he went along to the *Fleece* to have a pint or two—for the whisky had left him with a raging thirst—and perhaps a meat pie, sandwiches or whatever they had that he fancied. Well, let 'em stare. They looked sideways at him in the *Fleece* too. Well, let 'em. He was minding his business, let them mind theirs. But if they wanted a bloody argument, they could have a bloody argument. He told two chaps that, and they said they didn't want one, and then they left. There were several other chaps there, in the Tap Room, but they did nothing but give him a few looks. He gave them a few looks too. Bloody twerps.

Then he saw what seemed to him a friendly face. It was old, wrinkled, grinning. He had seen that face all his life but couldn't remember for the moment whose it was.

" Know you, don't I? " he mumbled. He didn't find it

122

easy to talk. Getting rusty in this bloody hole. Tongue didn't work.

"Yew do, yew do, Eddie," cried the old one, showing still more of his ancient gums. "Charlie—old Charlie Shuttle—from Four Elm Farm. Known yer since yer were that 'igh, lad."

"That's right," Eddie said. "Old Charlie—good old Charlie. 'Ave a drink with me, Charlie?"

"Well, thank yer," said the old man. "I don't mind if I takes a glass o' bitter."

"Yer'll 'ave a pint," said Eddie. Then he shouted · "Give Old Charlie a pint o' bitter—sharp!"

They didn't like that—there were more nasty looks—but they produced the pint.

"An' the best of 'ealth," said Old Charlie. "An' 'ow's yourself, Eddie, these stirring times?"

"I dunno, Charlie," Eddie said vaguely. "Just got back—see? I dunno 'ow I am yet. Not so bloody good, I fancy—no, not so bloody good."

The old man winked. "Yew got a bit of a load on this day, 'aven't yer, lad? Bin downing a few, eh?"

"That's right, Charlie. Not drunk, y'know. Don't you go sayin' I'm drunk now."

"No, no, Eddie." The old man chuckled. "Market style, I'd say—market style."

Eddie was not sure what this meant but he let it pass. Nothing suspicious and unfriendly about Old Charlie anyhow. Good Old Charlie! Then he remembered something about the old man that was important. "I know, Charlie," he cried triumphantly, "you work for the Kenfords—an' always 'ave done. That's it. That's it. 'Ere, 'ow's 'Erbert?"

Charlie gave him a wise old look over the top of his pint mug. "I've 'ad a talk or two with 'im—on the subjeck o' these war times an' so forth—an' 'e's doin' a bit o' quiet thinkin', 'e is. I sees it in 'is face. I set 'im a-thinkin '." And the old man chuckled complacently.

" It don't need you to set 'im thinkin'," said Eddie. "'Im an' me was out there together—see?—an' I know ' Erbert. Best bloody corporal we ever 'ad, 'Erbert Kenford was."

" A good steady lad," Old Charlie admitted. " We've 'ad many a talk in our time. Not like 'is brother—can't talk to '*im*. Knows it all, Muster Arthur does. Won't listen. But Muster 'Erbert'll listen—an' take notice too."

" An' another thing," Eddie continued, too much worried by some vague thought to bother about what the old man was saying, " there's enough 'ere to start any chap thinkin'. *I'm* thinkin'."

" About what, Eddie? "

Eddie frowned. This question came too early. He needed time to deal with this. " 'Bout everything, see? " he muttered. " Lot to think about, Charlie. Tryin' to get it straight—this an' that," he ended lamely.

Unfortunately one of the loudest mouths in Crowfield —Ernie Williams, the carter—now had to come butting in, just at the wrong moment. " See yer back, Eddie. All right, eh? Careful with that nice new civvy suit, boy. An' what's Old Charlie tellin' yer? "

Old Charlie, who did not like Ernie Williams, shrank a little, leaving any reply to Eddie.

" We're talkin' serious," said Eddie, frowning at this interruption.

" Yer look like it."

" Never mind what we look," cried Eddie aggressively. " You don't look so bloody marvellous, if it comes to that. An' just take yourself somewhere else."

" 'Ere yer don't own the bloody place, y'know."

" No, an' you don't neither."

As the two big fellows glared at each other Old Charlie

quietly retreated. "No use quarrelin', masters," he was saying, but neither of them heard him.

It was true that Eddie had never liked Ernie Williams and that they had had trouble before, years ago. It was also true that Eddie felt that sooner or later that day he would have to have a big flaming row with somebody. Nevertheless it did occur to him, in a vague and depressed fashion, as they both stood there glaring, waiting for the next move, that there was no sense in all this. It was all part of the vast mysterious wrongness of things.

Ernie Williams stepped back a pace, drank off his beer, then put his glass down. So Eddie finished his beer too, and put the pint mug on the nearest table. When he turned round again, Ernie Williams was waiting for him. And now Eddie forgot there was no sense in it. Suddenly he hated the sight of Ernie Williams' large meaty face.

"Yer'd better understand this," Ernie Williams was saying. "Yer might 'ave bin chuckin' your weight about in other places but you're not goin' to do it 'ere when I'm 'ere—see?"

"No?"

"No."

Maddened more by the sneering look on Ernie Williams' face than by anything that had been said, Eddie made a blundering rush at him, only to be stopped and severely jolted by a blow on the chest. This brought him out of his vagueness, his blurred sense of talking and acting in a dream, and sent him fighting mad. The landlady and her daughter started screaming ; the other chaps crowded round and tried to pull the two apart ; Ernie Williams managed to land a few blows ; but Eddie went tearing in, huge fists whirling, hammering and smashing, and soon Williams was a gasping bleeding ruin. Then, while the pub was still in an uproar, Eddie staggered out, dabbing at an eye that would be black before long. He made off blindly for his cottage.

He felt a touch on his arm. It was Old Charlie.

" 'Ad to keep out o' the way, Eddie," said the old man. " Ernie Williams don't like me nor me 'im, an' I'm long past takin' proper care o' meself in the way o' fist fighting." Then he chuckled. " Proper pastin' you give 'im though, boy, an' I never 'ope to see no better. Potted meat—that's what yew made of 'im—potted meat ! "

Eddie was not triumphant. " It didn't ought to 'ave 'appened though, Charlie," he muttered. " Didn't ought to 'ave 'appened. More trouble. More an' more trouble."

" That's 'ow it is," said Charlie solemnly. " An' that's 'ow it will be, Eddie, till there's more thinkin' done on all sides."

" The way it's goin'," Eddie continued, " I'll 'ave Parkinson comin' for me with a warrant this time. 'Ave to talk to somebody. I'm all in a muddle."

" I'll pass the word to Muster 'Erbert if 'e's at 'ome this day," said Charlie.

" Yes, you could do that," said Eddie mournfully. " Though it's Ser'nt Strete I ought to see."

Early that evening, sober now but looking rather battered and still feeling desperately confused, Eddie was turning down the side-road that led over the hill to Swansford. And it was there that he met Herbert Kenford.

" Eddie," cried Herbert, " what's the matter with you? "

Eddie shook his head. " A lot, 'Erbert."

" You've got a nasty eye. Ernie Williams, eh? Old Charlie told me."

" That's right. Ernie Williams. But that's not it, 'Erbert, that's not it."

Herbert looked at him with kindly concern. " What

is it then? What's the trouble, you old chump ? "

Eddie shook his head **again**. " Can't stop to talk, 'Erbert. Must see the Sarge. Must see 'im."

" Alan Strete? Is that where you're going now? He might not be there, Eddie."

" Got to chance it," Eddie mumbled. " Must see 'im. Got to tell 'im."

Herbert put a hand on his shoulder. " I've never seen you looking so down, Eddie. Come on, it's not as bad as all that."

" It's bad enough an' it can soon be worse," Eddie said, still shaking his head. " All gone wrong. I could be doin' bloody murder soon—honest I could."

" Eddie, I'd better come with you."

" Be all right if yer did, 'Erbert, but yer needn't, y'know. I mean to say——"

" No," said Herbert firmly, " I'm coming with you, Eddie. I want to see Alan Strete too. One or two things I want to talk over. So if you don't mind, I'll come too. All right to you? "

Eddie produced rather carefully the ghost of one of his old wide grins. " You an' me, Corporal Kenford, we'll go an' report to the Ser'nt. An' let's get cracking or something else'll start 'appenin' to me, an' next time I don't know what the 'ell I might do."

" Come on, then," said Herbert ; and they moved off. Eddie lumbered by his side in that old bear's walk that Herbert remembered so well. It was an evening of clear gold. The lane went winding here beneath festoons of lilac and laburnum. The hills seemed to have been cut out of gold-dusted green velvet. The sky was infinitely distant, pure, serene. It was an evening that seemed to belong to another life, not to them as they were now. Ironically it spread its beauty above their disenchantment.

" Just like that time at Syracuse," said Herbert, and

then, when Eddie made no reply: " Want to talk about it now, Eddie, or would you rather leave it till we see Alan Strete? "

"Let's leave it," said Eddie, lumbering on. "If' e's not there I'll try an' tell yer. But I 'ope to God 'e is. Didn't think I'd need the Sarge any more, but I was wrong, 'Erbert, I was wrong. I need 'im bloody bad."

" And I'm not sure I'm not in the same boat," said Herbert slowly.

" Why—you're all right, aren't yer? "

" I don't know about that, Eddie. Anyhow, I'm glad to see you. Meant to come along and see how you were doing. Heard you'd had a bit of trouble. But of course we don't know if Alan's there or what he may be doing or even if he'll want to see us. He may have had enough of us."

" Now yer don't believe that, do yer? " said Eddie anxiously.

" I don't want to. No, I don't believe it. Make a difference to me if he'd felt he'd done with us."

" Diff'rence! I don't know what it'ud do to me—the mess I'm in now. I bin sayin' to meself all day, 'You go an' see Ser'nt Strete, way yer used to do'. Can't do nothin' else now. Either that or I go off me rocker."

And it was then that they saw the car coming towards them, and Herbert, noticing who was in it, gave a shout and held up a hand.

8

" WHAT'S the matter with you this morning? " asked Diana suspiciously.

The question was all right. Diana had always been asking him what was the matter with him. What was new, different, deadly and wrong, was the suspicious tone. It was not part of the old sisterly anxiety, but a genuine suspicion, deeper and darker than anything the old Di had felt. Life had given her Derek and had then snatched him away from her, and now she didn't trust it an inch. Everybody, even Alan, might be a member of the Fifth Column.

"It's drink," said Alan lightly. "Booze or wollop. Last night his lordship did us very proud. Ask Gerald— he was shifting it too. Now nine times out of ten when you've been partaking so freely you wake up in the morning sober and sad, with the usual hangover. But now and again—perhaps not even once out of ten times, less than that—you wake up with a sort of carry-over, you're still rather gay and cock-eyed. And this," he concluded, " is one of those times. Strictly speaking, I'm still a bit tight."

" I don't believe it," she told him.

" I assure you, Di, that's how it is."

She eyed him gravely. " How was Betty? "

Good old Di, he thought, she can still drop one bang on the target. He would have to handle this carefully. "Dear Betty is still beautiful and idiotic. They put her next to me at dinner and she told me all about her husband."

" I'll bet she did."

" I'm going over there to lunch today," Alan announced very casually.

" Mother will be furious. Have you told her? "

Alan shook his head. " If she asks where I'm going, I'll tell her. But if she doesn't ask, then we'll leave it. And when I say ' we '——"

" Yes, I know what you mean," Diana interrupted, looking rather cross.

" I heard Gerald asking for her after somebody had

129

called him up on the telephone. He may have some bit of excitement that will keep her busy."

Diana looked at him speculatively. " She thinks you're going to do some job for that awful Lord Darrald."

" I might, y'know," said Alan airily. " I'm toying with the idea. Have to let 'em know this afternoon."

" You oughtn't to decide anything important today," said Diana shrewdly.

" Why not? "

" You're in a silly mood. Yes, you are, Alan. I know you."

Gerald marched in on them, grinning broadly. " The way you two sit gassing over the ruins of breakfast ! Well, we have a distinguished visitor this morning—looking in for a quick one about twelve, on his way over to Darrald's place for lunch. Buddin' statesman. Now Under-Secretary or something—for Imperial Collaboration. My old chum—Tubby Arncliff. Don't think you've met him , have you? "

No, they hadn't met him. " Who is he? " asked Alan.

" Tubby? Oh—his old man is Lord Bennervale, y'know. Tubby's the younger son. We were at school together and then at Sandhurst—very old pals. He was in my division too, early part of the war, and then he went down with something, put on his bowler hat and went into politics. Anyhow, he's looking in for a drink this morning. Have we any gin? "

" No, and we shan't have any until the end of next week," said Diana getting up.

" Uncle Rodney might have some—cached away."

" I don't think he has," said Diana, taking her tray, " and even if he had I don't believe he'd let us have any, You'll have to make do with sherry."

" It's a filthy sherry," said Gerald, going to open the door for her. " Can't imagine where the stuff comes from now. However, we'll see." He closed the door after Diana, then came back and looked rather anxiously at Alan, who was lighting his pipe.

" You goin' to be in when Tubby's here, old boy? "

" Depends. I'll have to push off soon after twelve. Why? "

" Well, if you are, just go easy with him, will you? He's not too bright—poor old Tubby isn't—and I don't want him to get a wrong impression of the family."

" But look here, Gerald—he's bright enough to represent His Majesty's Government on the all-important subject of Imperial Collaboration——"

" Yes, I know, old boy," said Gerald dubiously. " But that's just politics. Their lot has always gone in for politics, and so I suppose something had to be found for Tubby. He's a dam' nice fella—straight as a die and all that—but not too bright, let's face it. So go easy with him, old boy. None of your monkey-tricks. Everything in words of one syllable—and all that, eh? "

Alan grinned and then suddenly began laughing, laughing until the tears ran down his cheeks. Gerald laughed too, his large red face turning almost purple. And this continued for a minute or two.

" I don't know what the devil we're laughing at," said Gerald finally.

" I've been trying to explain to Di," Alan gasped, " only she doesn't understand. The fact is, I drank too much last night, and now this morning instead of the usual hangover I have a sort of carry-over—still feel a bit tight and light-hearted—you know——"

" Know exactly what you mean, old boy. Have had it myself, though not this morning. A couple of drinks —and you're off again. That was the trouble with poor old Jack Stowers—remember him? No, of course you wouldn't. But that was always poor old Jack's trouble.

Morning after was as bad as the night before. I remember——"

But Gerald had hardly launched himself into the strange saga of Jack Stowers when the postman was heard, and Alan went out to him. There was a parcel, obviously of gramophone records, for Uncle Rodney, and Alan took it upstairs.

Wearing an old but still magnificent wine-coloured dressing-gown, Uncle Rodney looked like a world-weary Roman emperor this morning. "Tiberius on Capri," Alan suggested.

"What about him?"

"You look like him,"

"I'm delighted to hear it," said Uncle Rodney. "If we'd had a Theatre for adults, somebody might have written a fine play about Tiberius. The contemporary notion that he retired to Capri to indulge in orgies is nonsense of course. He was quite capable of indulging himself up to the hilt in Rome, if he'd wanted to. Also I doubt if any sensible man ever plunged more than once into an orgy—he'd feel such a fool. No, Tiberius left Rome because he was bored with it, and that's what the solemn asses there couldn't forgive." He was now busy unpacking the records. "The Delius Violin Concerto. Golden twilight of farewell—and all that sort of thing. We'll play it shortly. Sit down, my boy. What's happening this morning?"

Alan explained about Tubby Arncliff, and repeated Gerald's warning about going easy with Tubby.

"Quite right, I imagine," said Uncle Rodney. "Don't know this young fella, but knew his father—Bennervale—at one time, and he always seemed to me half-witted. His wife—this fella's mother—she was a daughter of old Lord Glandestry—had an extraordinary passion for guardsmen—pick 'em up and smuggle 'em in at all hours.

132

Probably caught it from her nursemaid when she was young. No psycho-analysts then to explain it. But dashed awkward for the family, as you can imagine. No, I'd hardly expect this fella to be very bright. I'll come down and have a look at him."

"Have you any gin?"

"A drop. Why?"

"There isn't any downstairs. And Gerald says the sherry isn't much good. And I'd like a decent drink even if this Tubby Arncliff doesn't care what he drinks."

"Probably won't. But you shall have a drop. What happened last night out at Darrald's place? What did you make of the chap?"

Alan told him all about the night before, keeping it all light and easy in a manner that suited both his listener and his own mood. Uncle Rodney, who had been starved of this sort of thing lately, chuckled.

"You're very bright this morning, my boy. Seems to have done you good."

"Last night, don't forget, you called me dependable but dullish."

"Certainly," said Uncle Rodney coolly. "Did that to brisk you up a bit, my boy. Put you on your mettle. Seems to have worked too. I'd take his money, y'know."

"Darrald's? The job on his rag?"

"Yes. Of course you'll have to turn out a lot of vulgar muck—for garage hands and chambermaids. But that's the kind of world you'll have to live in, so you might as well take some easy money out of it. If there were some decent alternatives, I'd suggest 'em to you, but there aren't. And if it's a choice between gangsters and dupes, then you'd better join the gangsters. I would in your place. Though I thank God I'm not in your place. The Delius now, eh?"

They played the Concerto through. Alan listened

133

rather idly. He was not in the mood for music this morning. It was coming from too far away.

"Well, that's that," said Uncle Rodney, stirring. "I'll know more about it in a few days. But if I'm to get dressed—to have a look at this fella—I'd better start now. Turn that disgusting old bath on, will you, my boy? Takes half an hour to fill. And I won't forget the gin."

Partly in order to dodge his mother, Alan went out for a stroll. The morning fitted his prevailing mood so neatly that he might have ordered it. There was a light breeze, crisp sunlight, and sharply painted patches of colour everywhere. It was like sauntering in and out of a good 1912 Academy landscape—hills, fields, barns, hedges, all nicely indicated—good tone ; sound values ; bright English Impressionism ; no nonsense anywhere— sold at the end of the first week for three hundred and fifty guineas. And Alan amused himself by joining the artist and his friends at the Cafe Royal and afterwards crossing with several of them to Dieppe, where Sickert was very rude. This passed the time nicely and enabled him to avoid thinking about himself and his own affairs, which should now be allowed, he felt, to sprout and blossom as they pleased. Let the bright silly morning flower in its own fashion. He would not count the gold of the afternoon and evening until it fell into his hands.

An important car at the door. Voices—yes, from the drawing-room, which must have been frantically tidied up this very morning, specially for Tubby. Alan made a modest entrance into the long room, which looked quite charming if a trifle spectral. He was greeted by his mother in her hostess manner. Uncle Rodney was there, bland and immense, the retired diplomat again. No Diana, but Gerald and Ann of course, large and chummy, almost giving a party in some Officers' Club in some vague remote oriental Hills. And the guest, taking his sherry like a man.

The Under-Secretary to the Minister of Imperial Collaboration, the younger son of the Earl of Bennervale, M.P. (Con.) for Sludberry, and so not only the wise representative of all the anxious Sludberrians but also the hope—or the Under-hope—of millions of distant Canadians, Australians, New Zealanders, South Africans and the like, was tallish, plumpish, pinkish-and-goldish, and looked comfortable enough at first glance but then gave the impression that he was only just beginning to recover from some profound shock. He was nervously anxious to please but did not seem to know quite how to begin.

" My young brother, Alan," said Gerald, who was master of ceremonies. " Just out of the army, Tubby. Gin-and-bitters, old boy? "

" Yes please," said Alan quickly. Gerald, who was never niggardly, began pouring an enormous gin-and-bitters. Good for Gerald.

" Heard Gerald talk about you of course," said Tubby slowly, as if the Dominions might want to listen. " He and I are old pals, you know. I hear you dined with Lord Darrald last night."

" Yes," said Alan. " Cheers ! "

" Darrald wants him to do a job on one of his beastly little comic papers," said Uncle Rodney.

" Oh—I say," said Tubby, but smiling apologetically —he looked terrified of Uncle Rodney—" they're not as bad as all that, are they? "

" Certainly they are," said Uncle Rodney severely. " Like—like—inspecting a chambermaid's bedroom."

" How do you know? " said Ann in her best and brassiest manner, the talk of Bangalore.

Lady Strete gave a quick little glance round and wore the smile that announced that she was not in charge of the conversation and thought it somewhat out of control.

" Because I've some imagination," said Uncle Rodney. " But I'm probably being unfair to chambermaids, who neither attract me—in the manner you suggest—nor arouse in me any marked feelings of antipathy. But if Lord Darrald's aren't beastly little comic papers, then what are they? "

" The most powerful and influential examples we have of our free and unfettered Press," cried Alan in a mock-oratorical manner. He had swallowed half that enormous helping of gin at one go, and could feel the effects.

" Well, you know, you're right too—in a way," said Tubby carefully. " They have—er—very great influence indeed. And we've found them——" he hesitated, and looked round the room, like another Flaubert, for the exact, the triumphant word—" very useful. Darrald himself too. He's—er—very—er—co-operative."

" And I suppose you've got all sorts of plans and that sort of thing, eh, old boy? " said Gerald, contriving to look like a beaming earnest thinker.

" Your work must be very interesting, I'm sure," said Lady Strete.

" Oh—rather," said Tubby. " We simply have to—er—get together with the Dominions."

" Of course," said Ann or Gerald or Lady Strete or perhaps all three of them together.

" Why? " asked Alan.

" Have another drink, old boy," said Gerald hastily.

" Thanks, Gerald, I will," said Alan cheerfully.

Tubby looked relieved, but his relief did not last long.

" I think that's a fair question," said Uncle Rodney. " Why? "

" Well—er—it's pretty obvious—isn't it, sir? I mean—we've pulled together during the war—most of the Dominions have put up a jolly good show—and now we

—er—have to plan—er—to pull together in the Peace. Good of the Empire—and all that," Tubby murmured.

"Quite right," said Alan, who was now ready to say anything. And he looked at Uncle Rodney. "I don't believe you care about the good of the Empire."

"Oh you can't say that, Alan," his mother protested, knowing by instinct that some mischief was brewing. She gave Alan a quick warning look, then turned to Tubby. "I suppose it means a great deal of hard work for you." But she was too late.

"Certainly I don't," Uncle Rodney began, taking the floor. "Every time anybody's ever talked to me about the good of the Empire and our duty to preserve it, I've discovered they've been making something out of it. As I've never been in a position to make anything out of it, I see the matter in a different light. As for the colonies themselves—Dominions, if you like—they seem to me to exist in order to perpetuate the more unpleasant features of English life and character—the high teas, the woollen underclothing, the shop and chapel attitudes, the lack of wit and gaiety and genuine refinement, the humbug and hypocrisy. As I take no pleasure in frozen mutton and imitation Burgundy and other repulsive products, I can't be expected to be enthusiastic about their commercial enterprise. If they have ever sent us anything delicious or charming, then I've never had the good fortune to appreciate it. As for the people—with the exception of a pretty widow from Vancouver I ran into once at Antibes—I never remember meeting one o' them who didn't seem to me either colourless and negligi-'';' or distinctly repellent. And so I suspect, Arncliff," he concluded, looking down at him with amiable condescension, "that you're wasting your time. Have another glass of sherry."

There were protesting cries and indignant glances.

Poor Tubby, a bright pink now, could be heard stammering his own protest. " Oh, I say, sir—can't believe you're really serious. I mean to say—some of them are pretty awful, no doubt—but that's not the point—is it? I mean—we really have to get together, whatever we may think of them. I heard the P.M. himself say——"

But Alan was no longer listening. It was time for him to go, for he would have to walk over to the Southam's. The two large drinks and this idiotic little party, in which everybody seemed to be playing a role for comedy, had between them heightened and fixed his mood of the morning so that now he could rest on a high point of hilarious irresponsibility. He felt like one of the heroes—if you could call them that—of those bright successful novels of the between-wars period, one of those clever charming chaps, sensitive but heavily armoured by their lack of responsibility, who wandered from party to party, affair to affair, like visitors from another planet. Perhaps that was the only way to make this world endurable : to pretend you had arrived on it from another planet, to regard it as a colossal greenish-blue bubble, irridescent with folly, glittering with the prizes meant for those who could see an inch or two further than all the fools.

" I must go," he announced abruptly. He seized Tubby's still protesting hand. " Delighted to have met you, I really am," he said with some sincerity. And he was off before any questions could be asked, legging it over to Crowfield.

" You look peculiar," said Betty.

" I *am* peculiar," said Alan. " I had two enormous gins —in honour of Gerald's old pal, Tubby Arncliff, now a member of His Majesty's Government—God help it ! Then I legged it hard to be here in time. Then I see you. It all adds up."

" Have another drink. No ice, I'm afraid. What do I

look like today? "

She was wearing green and had piled her hair up high.
" Very exotic. Blonde Oriental. Something very fancy
and expensive imported by Kubla Khan—the talk of
Xanadu. An underwater touch too," he continued,
examining her gravely. " The strange woman from the
sea. In terms of Jung's Analytical Psychology—an
Anima figure."

" Darling," she said happily, " I haven't the least idea
what you're talking about. But you make it sound
exciting."

" It is exciting."

" It's more than lunch will be, I warn you. That'll
be foul. Isn't this place awful? "

He looked about him. " Very much like ours," he
said. " I wouldn't have thought that a few years ago,
but coming back to them, after being away some time,
I see that your place and ours are almost exactly alike.
They've both had it—so to speak—and they're both not
going anywhere, except to the dust-bin."

" Oh—it's not as bad as that," she protested, not understanding him.

" I meant something different." He glanced around
again. " Some charming things here really. We have
some too. But really they're both rather tatty museums."

" You ought to see my little cottage—I have one,
y'know—and it's sweet."

" All right. Invite me, Betty."

" You're invited, darling."

Their eyes met for a moment, and she smiled a slow
secret smile. He might talk the first nonsense that came
into his head about her being exotic and mysterious and
an Anima figure, but the fact remained that Betty could
be a very exciting creature. He felt the excitement now.

" Finish that and let's eat, such as it is," she cried gaily.

The dining-room was a darkish little room, full of re-
minders of Colonel Southam and the other Southams
before him, and Betty looked gorgeously out of place
in it. They were served by an elderly maid, who had
clearly taken a dislike to Betty some time ago and regarded this little party with disapproval. After a few
minutes Betty dismissed her.

"I told you the food would be foul," said Betty. "My
fault really. I meant to cook something for you myself
—you probably won't believe it, but I really can cook—
but I forgot and so didn't get up in time. I think I must
have been a bit tight last night."

"I'm still a bit tight," said Alan.

"It suits you. Some men are better when they're lit
up, and you're one of them. What are you doing today?"

"All I have to do today is to ring up that chap Markinch—you remember him, last night?—to tell him if I'm
taking that job they've offered me. He took a poor view
even of my thinking about it overnight, so I mustn't fail
to ring him."

"You can do that from here."

"I'd like to, if I may, Betty."

"You're going to take it of course. Tell me about it."

After he had explained what he was supposed to do
for them and how much they were ready to pay him, he
went on: "There wasn't any 'of course' about it last
night. I was very uncertain. But today I feel like
taking it."

"You'd be a chump if you didn't, darling."

"If Tubby can be Under-Secretary to the Minister of
Imperial Collaboration, then the least I can do, to add to
the comedy, is to write nonsense for the *Gazette*. If
we're all clowning, then I might as well make something
out of it. Then later on, perhaps, I can work my way
from the back row of the chorus up towards the front

row of comics. What's in this drink you've given me, my pet?"

"A lot of gin and some sort of imitation orange stuff. Just drink it and don't worry. What are you going to do after telephoning?"

"If you don't turn me out, I shall lean back somewhere and admire you, comparing you to a summer's day and so forth."

"All right then, I shan't turn you out. Rice pudding, d'you mind? I never touch it. I'll smoke, and then I needn't smoke later, when I'm a summer's day and so forth. What's an Anima figure?"

"It's a bit elaborate," said Alan, "and difficult with rice pudding."

"Don't bother then, but tell me sometime—I want to know. Don't think I haven't any brains at all. I know I'm lazy as hell, but I'm not a fool. No, I know you've never treated me like one. That's one of the things I like about you. No little woman stuff. Another thing, Alan," and she looked across at him solemnly, her curious eyes darker than usual, "you're more attractive than you used to be, now that you're older and a bit tougher. Do you know that?"

"No, but I'm delighted," said Alan, who really felt that he was. He smiled at her across the table. How desperate he had been about her once, when he was young and desperate! (Now—this moment anyhow—he felt gay but old.) "You know my Uncle Rodney, don't you? He'd appreciate you." And he began to tell her about Uncle Rodney.

Then she rose and said: "You'd better think about your telephoning, hadn't you?"

"Yes," he said, and walked round to her. She did not move but waited, bland and wide-eyed. He took her in his arms, with an even more delightful ease than the night before ; and her lips opened under his. Then she leaned away from him and gently pulled his arms down.

"Better telephone."

"I don't feel like telephoning," he muttered.

"But you must, darling. Besides, you can't start making love to me here—it isn't safe. Also, I have an idea."

"What is it? " He felt muzzy.

"Tell you later," she called back gaily, leading the way. "There's the telephone. I'll go and make the coffee —the stuff they do in the kitchen is awful muck."

He had to wait some time before he could get through to Lord Darrald's house. They were probably still ringing up Paris, Rome and Washington. Well, perhaps he would be doing it soon. He felt differently today about these people and their antics, almost on the inside with them. You stood outside, were sent here and there, were told to do this and that, and were immensely impressed ; but now he felt he knew how it was done. It was as easy as making love to Betty once you stopped taking her seriously and feeling desperate about her. When he finally did get through to Markinch, he was curt and rather offhand.

"Alan Strete here. About that job you offered me last night. Remember? "

"Yeh. Taking it? "

Alan nearly said "Yeh," too.

"Okay, Strete. We pay you thirty-five a week and reasonable expenses. Twelve weeks guaranteed—and you can sign your stories. See Farley at the office Tuesday or Wednesday. Better make it Tuesday. Okay? "

"Okay," said Alan, who felt that it was about time he began speaking their language. "I'll be at the *Gazette* on Tuesday."

"Fine ! After you'd gone last night, the Boss was ready

to bet you wouldn't take the job." Markinch chuckled. "This leaves me one up on him. Listen to Farley—though you'll probably want to kick his backside. He knows his job an' he can teach you yours. Be seein' you in London, Strete."

As easy as that. An introduction or two in the right quarters, a few chats over a few drinks, and then you were inside the ring too. And as he went off to find Betty, he felt a sudden and rather angry contempt for all the blank-faced millions who were outside, gaping and wondering, waiting to see how their lives would be shaped.

"Very good coffee," he told Betty.

"I said it would be. You wouldn't think it, but, as I told you before, I'm rather good around the house now if I want to be. Had to learn during the war. Was the job all right? And when do you start?"

"Have to report in Fleet Street on Tuesday."

"We ought to celebrate."

"All right. How—and where?"

She smiled her special smile, and he watched it appreciatively. "But look here," he told her, "don't come up from the mysterious green depths and give me that smile unless it means something."

"I was thinking," she said slowly. Then, after he had waited a few moments, she flashed across at him a wide, frank, wicked grin, quite irresistible.

"Whatever that means I say 'Yes, certainly,' Betty."

"Look, darling, I was thinking about celebrating. Let's go on a binge. I was going down to my cottage anyhow today—I've bagged the car too until Tuesday—so what about coming with me? Then you can go to town on Tuesday and I come back here. Just ourselves. There's quite a good pub—food and drink, if we want it —on the main road only about a mile and a half away.

We can have lots of fun. And you deserve some, and so do I. Um?"

He nodded, smiled at her, then went over and gently tilted her face. "One—and then stop," she murmured. "It really isn't safe here. Wait until we get down there."

When he returned to his chair, trembling a little, he filled his pipe with enormous deliberation. "I'll have to slip back home and put a few things in a suitcase. When do we go?"

"After tea, I suggest," she replied. "Half-past five— or six-ish. Look, I'll drive you over, lurk round the corner while you get your bag, and then off we go. Only takes about an hour or so. And it's a heavenly little place, darling. Now talk to me quietly. Tell me what I'm really like. You're the only one who can talk to me properly."

So all afternoon he stared across at the exquisite mask of her face, often curved in a tiny secret smile, and mostly talked nonsense, not a word of which he could have remembered afterwards. On idle talk and long level glances the afternoon slipped by like a dream, although somewhere behind the dream a pulse was beating, his blood was checking the hours. Tea came and went and was no more than a shadow moving across a wall. "We might have been sitting in the Summer Palace of some forgotten Chinese Emperor," he said.

She smiled, then jumped up, all energy and purpose. "Time to go. Help me to put some things in the car."

She stopped the car, to wait for him, about a couple of hundred yards from the entrance to the drive of Swansford Manor. There was nobody about. "Hurry up. No family chats or anything. If I'm spotted, I shall say I'm giving you a lift to the station."

"Shan't be more than five minutes," he promised her, and hurried up the drive. Nobody in the hall. He ran up to his room, flung some things into a small suitcase, then carried it out—only to run into Diana at the top of the stairs.

" Where are you going? "

" I've accepted that job on the *Gazette*. Have to report at the office." He disliked lying to Diana and this was the best he could do.

" Tonight? Where are you going to stay? "

" I don't know. That doesn't matter."

She looked hard at him. " You're up to something, Alan." She stepped back, knowing that he was in a hurry. " All right. Go on. You needn't tell me." She was no longer accusing him now. She was despairingly resigned, almost hopeless. She had retreated, not one step but a long way. She even looked smaller, older, defeated.

None of this belonged to the world he had been living in all day. As if a nerve had been pressed, he suddenly ached with pity. " I can't tell you now, Di," he said gently. " It's been a queer day. I'll tell you all about it soon. We haven't talked properly yet, have we? Just wait, and we will. Don't look like that, please, Di. You're not beaten."

Then he ran downstairs, as if today's bubble of a world had gone floating ahead and he must run to jump back into it. Nobody downstairs again. He rushed down the drive. Betty had the door open ready for him.

" We'll have to go back along the Crowfield road," she said as they moved off, " and then turn into the Bancester road. Shouldn't be much traffic. We'll be there in an hour or so." She began singing in a queer tuneless little voice she had, a voice much younger and more unformed than the rest of her, as if it had never caught up. Something rather touching about it ; but not quite right now. Rather like what he had just felt about Diana.

" I'm beginning to feel rather gay," said Betty.

" I've been gay all day," he said, " and now I'm steadily getting gayer." But was he? He told himself firmly that he was. And then he saw them coming along the road. A grey suit, a brown suit. Herbert Kenford and Eddie Mold.

" Betty, stop, stop ! " he shouted.

" Why, what's the matter? "

" These two chaps—they may be wanting to see me. You must stop."

" Oh, all right," she said crossly, pulling the car up only a few yards from them. " Only—hurry up—and be careful what you say. One of them knows my father. And do cut it short, whatever it is."

The two had stopped, after Herbert had shouted and held up his hand, and now Alan went up to them.

" Hello, chaps ! Were you coming to see me? " He saw that Eddie looked as he'd been in a scrap recently and that Herbert was looking even more serious and determined than usual. And he guessed then that this was something more than a friendly visit.

" Yes," said Herbert. " Eddie here wanted to see you very badly——"

" Just 'ad to see you, Ser'nt," Eddie muttered, giving Alan a sudden desperate look of appeal, " or I'll be doin' bloody murder——"

" And I wanted to see you too," Herbert continued, " and so I came over with him. But you're off somewhere, are you? "

" Yes. What's been happening? " And he looked at Eddie.

" Well, I can't tell it all now," said Eddie in a low voice. " Started with some trouble I 'ad with the wife. She'd bin goin' with some Yanks while I was away—an' everybody knew—but that's only the start. I'm all muddled up—an' a bit bloody desp'rate an' that's fact."

" And what about you, Herbert? "

146

Herbert smiled rather grimly. " I'm not so bad as poor old Eddie here, but I think I'm all muddled up—and a bit bloody desperate too. That's why we wanted to talk to you, Alan. But if we can't, then we can't."

They both looked at him, and he knew that look. He had seen it many times before, often in very nasty places ; and for a moment he seemed to be back in the sweat and reek of battle. And he knew now what he had to do. " If it comes to that, I'm all muddled up too. We'll have to have a talk about it, won't we? "

" That's right, Sern't," said Eddie with immense relief.

" Well, just a minute, chaps," said Alan. " Then I'll be with you."

" You look queer," said Betty, holding the door open. " What's the matter? "

" I'm sorry, Betty," he said very quietly. " I can't make it. I must stay and talk to these chaps."

" Why on earth should you? " She was furious. " My God, you don't mean to say you're ditching me——'

" I'm sorry. But I must. You see, we were all at the front together——"

" I don't care where you were," she cried angrily. " I only know this finishes you with me. Here—take your damned bag."

The car went charging straight at Herbert and Eddie, who had to jump smartly to avoid it, and then it hooted furiously and was gone. Alan picked up his suitcase. The other two joined him.

" As I'm landed with this case," Alan said, grinning rather self-consciously, " I think we'd better go along to my place so that I can get rid of it. There's an old summerhouse at the end of the garden, and we might sit there until it gets too cold—eh? After that we can go indoors and talk. I have an idea we may have a good deal to say. So let's get going."

9

" ANYBODY want any beer? " Alan asked. " There ought to be some up in the house."

" Not for me, thanks," said Eddie. " I've 'ad more than my share this last day or two."

" I don't want any, thanks, Alan," said Herbert, who sounded rather dreamy. He stared out of the summer-house, where they were sitting in dilapidated deck-chairs. " Nice here, isn't it? "

They looked through a little gap at the stream and the bright water-meadows, at the sedges and rushes, the thick old thorns and the delicate willows ; and everything there seemed to be illuminated and yet partly hidden by the gold gauze of the evening. It was all old and familiar and yet had at this moment the radiance and enchantment of some promised land. They were deeply aware of it all the time they were talking.

" Well, Eddie," said Alan quietly, " what happened? Want to tell us? "

" Yes I do," replied Eddie, " if I can get it straight." Very carefully he began his story, from the moment he reached home and found his telegram on the floor. The words did not come easily but he made them understand all that had happened to him.

" Mind yer," he concluded, " I'm not blaimin' nobody, not even the wife now. An' I kept losin' me temper—specially when I'd 'ad some beer—an' I suppose I oughtn't to 'ave done. But they got me down, the whole bloody lot of 'em. An' if it's goin' on like this, Sarge, I don't know what I'll be doin' to somebody soon. Seems to me I'd better ask 'em to take me back into the army. I thought I was comin' 'ome, but I seem to 'ave arrived somewhere else. I'm all in a bloody muddle. Is it me

148

or is it them? If it's me, what do I do? An' if it's them, what's the matter with 'em? "

Nobody spoke for a few moments. Herbert gave Alan a questioning glance. Eddie kept his dark battered face turned away.

" Eddie," said Alan gently, " can I ask you something?"

" Yer can ask me anything, chum. What is it? "

" It's about you and your wife, you see," said Alan with some hesitation. " Suppose it had just been between you two—you'd found out what she'd done, but nobody else knew—would you have forgiven her? "

" Well, she didn't ought to 'ave done it, y'know," said Eddie earnestly, " not with me out there, she oughtn't. Not right, is it? But there was the kid and all that, same as Fred Roseberry's wife said. One thing an' another . . ."

" And you can easily get into a state of mind," said Alan, who was remembering too much and trying not to show it, " when nothing's very real and important and it doesn't seem to matter much what you do. Just as if you're tight."

" Well, I might 'ave given 'er a good talking to, an' then said, ' Let's forget it.' I might 'ave done that," said Eddie.

" If you ask me, Eddie," said Herbert quietly, " that's really what you want to do anyhow. And I fancy it's on your conscience a bit."

Eddie considered this carefully. " Yer might be right, 'Erbert," he admitted.

" I think he is, y'know," said Alan.

" I want to do what's right," said Eddie. " An' if that's what's right, I'll do it. But we can't live round 'ere no more. And any'ow I don't want to. What's the matter with 'em round 'ere—tell me that."

" I think I can tell you that," said Alan. " You come out of the army, where you've been with chaps you've got to know very well and you've all been doing a job together that you all understand. Right? Well, the point is, these people aren't like that. They were once perhaps—y'know, after Dunkirk and all the time they thought we might be invaded. But when the feeling of danger that brought them together had gone, they began to separate themselves again, and perhaps pulled a bit harder away just because they had had to keep in line for a time. They're not very different now from what they were before the war. But you are—and that's the point. And you were expecting something that isn't there. And when most of 'em talk about your settling down, as they call it, they mean you must stop expecting anything very different."

"An' 'ave I to? I mean, do I just shake down with 'em, best I can, or what?"

"No, you don't," said Herbert quite fiercely. This was so unlike Herbert that the others stared at him in surprise. He looked embarrassed. "I think Alan's right. But they're not all like that. Some of 'em understand what we're feeling. They're on our side. Somebody said to me that whatever I did I mustn't go back on what I was feeling now, that I mustn't let them make me comfortable and stop me thinking and persuade me that now we can go on in the same old way, not caring what happens to other people. She—this person—said we're all tied up together now, whether we like it or not, and that if we aren't all working and thinking for each other, it'll all go on being hate and misery and bloody murder."

Eddie stared. "Nobody's talked like that to me. An' all sorts 'ave 'ad a go at me—manager an' parson an' policeman—all sorts."

"Who was this, Herbert?" asked Alan.

Herbert looked confused. "It was a girl. As a matter of fact, it was that girl from the aircraft factory who

150

argued with us in the pub at Lambury."

Eddie was astonished. "Yer mean that dark, good-lookin' Judy who was talkin' out of 'er turn?"

"Yes, except she wasn't really. Her name was Doris Morgan, remember? And she'd said one or two things to me that—er—well, interested me, and last night I had a long talk with her. She's a fine girl that." He looked at them defiantly.

Alan grinned. "I thought so the other afternoon. Bit fierce and not quite my style, but just right for you, Herbert, and do you good. And she said all that, did she?"

"Yes, and a good deal more. And I think she might do me good. She can certainly try. I'm seeing her to-morrow. But it's—difficult."

"What's difficult about it? Come on, Herbert, you might as well tell us now. And don't look so embarrassed about it. Eddie and I have been through it in our time."

"That's right," said Eddie, producing this first grin.

"Though I don't know where I am yet," Alan continued. "I'm still acting the goat."

"Wasn't that Colonel Southam's daughter who was in that car?" And Herbert gave him a shrewd look.

"Yes, but forget it. And anyhow we're talking about you and your girl friend now. What's difficult about it?"

"Well, it's early days yet, of course," Herbert began rather gloomily, "but so far it does look depressing. She belongs to factories and towns and all that. I belong to the country. If she comes with me, she's lost. If I go with her, I'm lost. At least, that's how it looks to us at the moment."

"I get it," said Eddie with solemn sympathy. "You're right too, 'Erbert. Nice little piece, but I don't see 'er gettin' up at 'alf-past five or bakin' pies an' pasties for a dozen 'aymakers."

"Wait a minute," cried Alan. "To start with, if she's worked in that factory, I'll bet she's got up at all hours and done a damned hard shift too. And I don't believe in this town-versus-country stuff. It's old-fashioned. We've got factories miles out in the country, and we'll have to keep 'em. And we'll have to have farms on the edges of towns too. So settle it between you. I think you're making a fuss about nothing. But how did you come to be talking to her like that, Herbert? I thought you'd be the one who would be settling down comfortably, back on the farm with nothing to worry about. What's happened to you?"

No longer shy now, Herbert told them about the supper on Thursday night and what he had felt afterwards. "I don't want you to feel I'm running down my own folks," he said finally. "I'm fond of them. They'd been planning for me, they'd been kind to me, and I couldn't help feeling I was ungrateful in a way. But I knew it was all wrong, just as Doris said. Mind you, as I told her, it's easy to get self-centred when you're farming. It's hard work and you're cut off from most other people and don't know what their lives are like. But it's no use, we can't go on like that. As Doris says, if you cut yourself off, then you begin to die. The war had to show us that, though it oughtn't to have been necessary. I couldn't stand hearing my father and brother talking as if nobody else mattered but our family, and that all we had to do was to grab our bits of land and farm them and then get as much out of everybody else as we could. We've had all that before—and look where it got us."

"What do you want then, Herbert?" Alan asked. "Collective farms?"

"I don't know what I want yet, Alan," said Herbert. "Haven't had time to think about it properly. Don't know enough yet. I'm going to try and find out what'll work the best. But that's the point. Not what suits us best, in our little corner, but what's best for everybody. Farming is what I know, so I'd like to do that, but I don't care whether I run my own farm or join with other chaps in some sort of agricultural co-operative or go and work on a collective farm, Russian style. What I can't stand any longer, not after what we've been through, is all this old stupid greedy grabbing and screaming, like a lot of half-starved dogs round a lump of horse meat. I didn't come back for that, didn't go away to fight for it, and if that's how people are going to behave here, now they're out of danger, then I'd rather go and start again in some other country. But I don't want to do that. I'd rather stay here and help to pull this country through. It's been worth fighting for, so now we've got to see it's worth living in."

"That's right," said Eddie. "But is it us blokes who've bin in the army that'll 'ave it to do?"

"No," said Alan, "that wouldn't work out right. Fascist touch there, eh Herbert?"

"Yes, no good," said Herbert. "Besides, plenty of chaps who've been in the army don't see it right. You've heard 'em talking. And other people, who haven't been near the army, feel just as we do."

"His Doris," Alan reminded Eddie.

"She's not my Doris, but she's one—certainly. That's what started her off the other day in the pub. I can talk to her just as I can to you two."

"Then you're bloody lucky," Eddie muttered, "an' you'd better stick to 'er. Never mind where you're goin' to live."

They said no more for a minute or two. The gold haze had deepened and there was blue, a hint of night, in the long shadows. The green of the water-meadows was fading. Sometimes the stream flashed white, coldly.

Alan shivered a little. " Want to go in now? "

" Not if you don't," said Herbert.

" I'm all right," said Eddie. " Suits me out 'ere."

" Then we'll stay out a little longer," said Alan. " And now I suppose you'd like to know about me. Well, you were just in time tonight. I was just about to behave—or to continue behaving—like a damned idiot. I was riding off, with a binge on the way, to take a job I'd been offered on the *Gazette*. This is what has happened." And he described the dinner-party at Lord Darrald's, and then sketched the talk he had had with Darrald and Markinch. Leaving Betty out, he went on to tell them how he had telephoned that afternoon to accept the job.

" I don't understand this, Alan," said Herbert rather severely. " You couldn't have worked for those people. You know the sort of stuff they'd have wanted you to write? "

" Yes, I knew. Probably when it came to the point, I couldn't have written it. But I have to explain why I took it on and why you saw me pushing off in that car."

" Needn't if yer don't want to," said Eddie. " It's all right by me. I know you'd never let anybody down. So does 'Erbert 'ere."

" No, I have to explain," said Alan. Steadily. " I have to explain to myself as well as to you. That's why I may have to go slow." As if to give himself time, he lit his pipe and watched the smoke curl away from it.

" You two came back to something different from what you expected. Perhaps you, Herbert, not so much as old Eddie here, but then that girl did something to you, Herbert, that helped a lot. Now what happened to me? I came back here—to what? Well, really to a kind of lunacy. I have an old uncle here—he's a fantastic museum piece but no fool—and he told me what it was —disintegration, sheer disintegration. The class they belong to, their kind of society, is simply dropping to pieces. They're all at the end of little blind alleys. They all accuse each other of being barmy—and they're right. There isn't anything more for them to do as a special class, but they can't—or won't—come out into the main road with the crowd and go somewhere. So they stay where they are—and quietly, decently, go mad. I had to pretend to myself that it didn't matter much and was rather funny. Then, I suppose in order to keep this pretence going, I had to persuade myself that nothing mattered much and that everything was a rather bad joke. It's not difficult to do that, particularly if you have a few drinks and keep your eye on a nice tempting wench."

"Like that piece in the car," said Eddie. "I saw 'er. Nasty temper she 'ad though."

"But wait a minute," said Herbert. "Where do Lord Thingummy—Darrald—and the *Gazette* come into this? Don't tell me those chaps are mad."

"Strictly speaking they are," said Alan. "But not in the same way. They've plenty to do and know what they're doing—up to a point. They've got power and they mean to keep it, until we give them a damned bad fright. But you can see why I fell for it, in my own little way, can't you? After seeing people you've known all your life, people close to you, hanging about at dead ends, muttering rubbish to themselves, it's exhilarating and tempting to meet some other people who think they know what they're doing and where they're going. If everything begins to look like a mixture of a bad joke and a racket, you feel you might as well be in on the racket. There was a chump here this morning—an old pal of my brother's—who's got into politics because his family has always been political, and he's already an under-secretary, and before we know where we are or he collects any brains, he may be a cabinet minister. Well, he didn't do me any good either. You must either fall in line with him, in the hope of grabbing what you can for yourself, or stand up and denounce him and all the people who put him where he is."

"Well, that suits me," said Herbert. "What's wrong with standing up and telling him where he can go?"

"Nothing," cried Alan. "And I'm ready to do it when you are. But I didn't see it like that this morning. It just didn't seem worth it. All a roaring farce anyhow— that's how I felt."

"Life's serious," said Herbert. "It's all we've got, and we can't afford to monkey with it."

Eddie grinned. "Always was serious to you, wasn't it, 'Erbert?"

"Yes, and it didn't seem so dam' funny to you when I met you tonight, Eddie," said Herbert, with a flash of temper. "You're only talking like that because now you feel better."

"That's right, I feel better," said Eddie, and added apologetically: "Just pulling your leg, 'Erbert. You're quite right. Get me, chum?"

"But you do see what I mean, Herbert?" Alan said earnestly. "Just remember, you came up against something quite different, not the kind of futility and gentlemanly daftness I found here. All half-dressed and nowhere to go. Hoping against hope that time will turn back for them, that next week might suddenly find itself in Nineteen Hundred and Five. Cutting themselves off from the trunk and the roots and the sap, and so beginning to die. I can't stay with them. I knew that. And now of course—now that I've come to my senses—I realise I can't go and write nonsense for Darrald and his pals, who know that most people tend to be rather stupid, short-sighted and lazy minded, and so they propose to do everything they can to make them more so."

"That's the game, is it?" said Herbert.

"That's it. And I was nearly in it, though I wouldn't have lasted long. Well, I can't go there. I can't stay here. I don't want to cheat and I don't want to rot. So what do I do?"

"Doris said 'Fight' and I see now she's right," cried Herbert. "We've done a lot of fighting——"

"Enough to last me," said Eddie drily.

"Is it? You've been fighting half the village——"

"'Ere, that's diff'rent."

"I know it is. I'm not talking about losing your temper in pubs," said Herbert sharply. "Fight for something worth fighting for."

"An' I say I've 'ad enough to last me for a bit," said Eddie, setting his jaw. If Herbert could be sharp, then Eddie could be obstinate. "I come back for some peace an' quiet, an' what I complain of is that I 'aven't 'ad it an' don't look like getting it."

The silence that followed was broken by a woman's voice.

Alan jumped up, surprised. "Diana!" The other two men rose too, staring at her in the dusk.

"I'm sorry," she told them. "I'm Alan's sister."

"This is Herbert Kenford," said Alan, "and this is Eddie Mold. We were all overseas together and came back together—I told you, remember?"

"Yes," she said. "I've been listening to you for the last few minutes. I didn't mean to, but I heard voices—and knew it couldn't be the rest of the family because they've gone out to dinner—and I thought you'd gone away, Alan—so I came up quietly, wondering who it could be, and then I didn't like to interrupt at once—so I had to listen. I'm sorry—if you mind my hearing what you said."

157

"No we don't," said Alan. "In fact, I'm rather glad."

"You didn't mention me," said Diana gravely, "and I can't pretend I'm sorry you didn't. But I came into it, didn't I?"

"Yes, you came into it, Di," Alan replied. "You remember what you said yesterday morning—about wanting to do something and wishing you liked people more?"

"Yes, of course." She looked at the other two, who were still shy and silent. "I lost my husband, who was in the Air Force. And since then it's been difficult for me. I haven't known what to do. I told Alan I couldn't stay here much longer. We talked about that yesterday." Her voice trembled a little. "Then Alan seemed different, and I was very worried—we've always talked and shared things. Now I know why you seemed different, Alan, and I feel a lot better. I hated it when you ran downstairs tonight with your bag. I knew something was wrong."

"So did I," he admitted, "though I tried hard to pretend to myself that I didn't. That's when the game I was playing didn't look so good. Then down the road I met Herbert and Eddie, who wanted to talk to me. I knew I couldn't go then. Sorry to have made you miserable, Di."

She smiled and shook her head. They did not speak for a few moments; a little group in the immense dusk. They could hear the splashing gurgling of the stream and the last bird calls.

"I gathered," said Diana with some hesitation, "that you all feel disappointed—dissatisfied—rather unhappy. But it seemed to be for quite different reasons. And perhaps it's simply because you all expected too much, which of course is quite natural. But—and I hate to sound depressing, but I must say it—there doesn't seem

158

to be anything you all want to do about it, something you can all do together."

"We've got to find out about that," said Alan slowly. "Remember, we don't know much yet. All we know for certain is what we've learnt in the last few days. For instance, I know that our class can't survive as a class and should stop trying. It doesn't matter about the old chaps like Uncle Rodney, who's just a fantastic survival. He may not do anybody much good, but he doesn't do much harm, unlike such brigands as Darrald and his lot. But I'm certain now that if we younger ones try to keep ourselves separate, we'll rot and die on our feet."

"I wonder," she said. Then she looked at Herbert. "This girl you know—I'd like to meet her—to talk to her."

"You'd probably dislike her at first," said Herbert, "and she'd probably dislike you——"

"I know. I'd be prepared for that—or I'd try to be. But I want to talk to another woman. She'd understand certain things——"

As her voice trailed away, Eddie took courage. "I've 'ad trouble with the wife. We 'ad a kid that died sudden, an' that upset 'er like. I wish yer'd 'ave a talk to 'er—for me——" And now his voice trailed away too.

"Yes, I will, if you think it would help." Then impulsively, she turned to Alan. "You say we're finished. But this doesn't look like it. These two came to you. Mr. Mold wants me to talk to his wife. That doesn't suggest we're useless."

"We're not useless, we're not finished," said Alan, "if we don't separate ourselves. After all we're people too. Some of us—like you, Di—are particularly nice people. But we must think of ourselves just as people. We must go along the main road and not crawl up blind alleys. We mustn't try to save something special for ourselves that the mass of people mustn't have. That's the mistake the collaborators made in the occupied countries—and we saw some of 'em being carted off, didn't we, Herbert? They joined hands with death simply to try and keep something for themselves. They thought they were being cunning and playing safe. And that's what too many people are still doing. And I see now that it can't be done. You can't make yourself safe any more."

"No, you can't," said Herbert. "Or if you can, you oughtn't to try. I felt it the other night when my father was talking. That's what was wrong."

"They were doing their best for you," said Diana, who could see them at the farm, planning for the son's return.

"I know they were," Herbert admitted. "That's what hurt. But it isn't good enough, you see. A lot of families and little groups of people, trying to make their bit safe for themselves—and never mind anybody else, that won't work any more. We've had that."

"He's right," said Alan. "We can't plan just for ourselves any longer. We're all in one big boat now and either we pull all together for the nearest shore or down we go."

"Down where?" asked Eddie. He was genuinely bewildered and was not trying to be funny.

"Look, Eddie," said Alan, "if we try to go on in the same old way—competing and grabbing and scrapping, trying to make the same rotten old formulas work, then we'll have huge slumps, unemployment, semi-starvation again. People will soon be bitter and angry. The fight for markets will be fiercer than ever. That means more wars, more bloody revolutions, and probably more mad dictators. Then very soon we'll all be half-starved and half-crazy, living underground and making thousand-ton rockets."

"Not for me, chum," cried Eddie. "I'd rather be underground for good, out of it, just pushin' the daisies up. But listen—people's got more sense than that."

"They ought to have," said Diana doubtfully.

"Before they know where they are, people find themselves clamped into situations by sheer force of circumstance." Alan waited a moment. "If you'd told people twenty-five years ago what was in store for them by Nineteen-Forty, they'd have laughed at you. But it happened."

"Well, are we barmy or what?" Eddie's voice, in his bewilderment and exasperation, rose almost to a squeak. "Look at me. I do my share o' fightin' an' then all I want is to come 'ome an' be quiet for a bit. And there isn't no 'ome an' I can't be quiet."

"It's hard luck," said Alan. "But you'll have to make a home. We'll all have to make one. We'll have to make this earth into a home. It's never been properly tried yet. Eddie, we've got to get cracking again."

"I dare say," said Eddie, rubbing his chin. "But it seems to me you blokes—now you're out—think better o' this army kind o' life than I do. I've 'ad enough of it. I want something diff'rent, I do."

"We all do," cried Herbert impatiently. "But for all that, this coming home—with everything in its favour—hasn't given us what we thought it would. Otherwise we wouldn't be here—beefing again. Something's wrong then. And soldiering, bad as it was, led us to expect something better. That's the point. Eh, Alan?"

Alan nodded but did not reply for a moment or two. He stared out at the fading hillside. When he did speak, he began very slowly. "Armies are huge machines that don't make anything. You move in them from one piece of destruction to another. But if it's the right kind of army, there's something good inside it, working between men and men. You do at least move together towards one common objective. It's better than civvy life has been up to now. Nobody tampers with the orders so that he can run a yacht or own a deer forest. Nobody sells the signals to keep control of a newspaper or a bank. Nobody surrenders a strong point for the sake of an expensive mistress or a collection of antique furniture. That's one difference."

"They'd be shot if they tried it," said Eddie.

"Well, it might come to that," Herbert growled.

"It needn't," said Alan. "If we can work together to destroy and to kill, then surely to God we can work together to build up and to create new life. If we can't, then we shan't last much longer. We have the choice—it stares us in the face now. Just as we had in Nineteen-Forty. Then we had to choose between asking for terms and perhaps saving something for a little while—and going on, alone, risking everything and everybody here in order to save everything and everybody everywhere. We made the choice. And what we did was so right that you could feel the strength of it in the very air. We behaved then like a great people. We have another choice now. Are we going to behave again like a great people—or to sink into obscurity, yapping and scrapping?"

"But Alan," Diana protested, "it isn't the same. After Dunkirk it was a perfectly simple choice that everybody could understand. Britain could give in or go on fighting. That's easy to decide. But this other choice you talk about—well, it isn't simple like that. What do we do? You don't know yourself."

"I know what we don't do," said Herbert sharply, "and that's something to start with."

"Yes," cried Alan, "we don't do what so many people seem to be doing already, before the blood's dry on the ground. We don't try to return to the muddle of the pre-war time. We don't go on thinking and behaving in the same old way. If it was disastrous before, it'll be disastrous again. We don't want the same kind of men looking after our affairs. We act as if we've learnt something. We don't keep shouting ' That's mine—clear off. We don't try to make our little corner safe—and to hell with anybody else ! We don't talk about liberty when what we really mean is a chance to fleece the public. We don't go back on all we said when the country was in danger. We stop trying for some easy money. We do an honest job of work for the community for what the community thinks we're worth. We stop being lazy and stupid, greedy and callous. We try to remember that it's much more important—and much more fun—to create than to possess. It's also much better to live uncomfortably, on short rations, as the Russians did, in a society that knows what it's doing and where it's going, than it is to lead a luxurious existence—for a little while —in a society that's wobbling from one disaster to the next. Instead of guessing and grabbing, we plan. Instead of competing, we co-operate. We come out of the nursery—and begin to grow up."

Alan was now on his feet, erect, towering, almost transfigured, and he stared into the dusk as if it held a vast invisible audience.

" Somebody once wrote—I think it was Heine," he continued, " that every epoch is a Sphinx, which plunges into the abyss as soon as its problem is solved. And I know now what our problem is. It isn't how to produce a few brilliantly gifted individuals, how to procure for one small class the utmost luxury and refinement, how to give enormous power to a few groups, how to produce two or three colossal monuments of art or learning. Modern man is essentially co-operative and communal man. What we do best—and better than men have ever done in earlier ages—is never something that an individual can do but always something that men have to

163

create together. And our problem, which we must solve or the Sphinx will destroy us, is how to use this power of working together for the benefit of the largest possible common human denominator. There's something in us now that will not rest nor find any lasting satisfaction while most human beings still exist in poverty, ignorance and despair. We have to make the round earth our home. We have at last to have faith in people, compassion for people, whether they have white faces, brown faces or black faces. This hope of a home on earth, this faith and this compassion are now at the very centre of our lives. If we're moved by them, if we base all our actions on them, we begin to live, drawing strength from the waters of life. But if we pretend they aren't there, if we try to ignore the great task, then we cheat ourselves into cruelty and murder, sink into madness, turn into stone. And—by Heaven!—politics, economics, psychology, philosophy, religion—though they still speak with different voices, they all look the same way now. This is the choice. Either the earth must soon be the miserable grave of our species or it must be at last our home, where men can live at peace and can work for other men's happiness."

" Whoa, steady on," cried Eddie. " Yer'll be either preachin' or in Parlyment next."

" And why shouldn't he be? " cried Diana. And there was new life in her voice.

Alan laughed. " Di, is there anything to eat? "

" As usual, not much. But I could make some tea and cut some sandwiches for you."

" I'll do the sandwiches," said Alan. " You brew up, Di. Come on chaps." And he led the way across the darkening garden towards the open door of the house and its welcome glow.

THE END